The Treasury of
Fairy Stories

The Treasury of Fairy Stories

Retold by Janet Barber

Contents

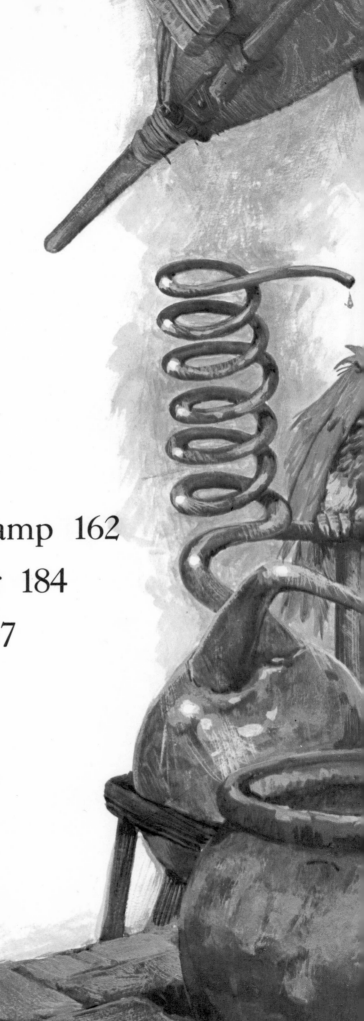

Snow White 6
The Brothers Grimm

The Lion and the Joiner 44
Arabian folktale

Abdullah from the Land and Abdullah from the Sea 68
1001 Nights

The Little Golden Fish 92
Russian folktale

The Three Little Pigs 116
English folktale

The Seven Ravens 140
The Brothers Grimm

Aladdin and the Wonderful Lamp 162
1001 Nights

The Ant and the Grasshopper 184
La Fontaine

The Hare and the Tortoise 187
La Fontaine

The Country Mouse and the Town Mouse 190
La Fontaine

The Rabbit, the Weasel and the Cat 193
La Fontaine

The Snow Queen 196
Hans Christian Andersen

Nawarana and the Giant 204
Eskimo folktale

The illustrations were drawn by the
following artists:

Lima: pages 6-43
Sergio: pages 44-67, 140-161
Ferri: pages 68-91
Una: pages 92-115
L'Alpino: pages 116-139
Enrico: pages 162-183
P. Nardini: pages 184-195
Benvenuti: pages 196-203
Gianni: pages 204-208

First published 1978 by
Octopus Books Limited
59 Grosvenor Street
London W1

ISBN 0 7064 0740 7

Produced by Boondoggle Limited
600A Commercial Road
London E1

Printed in Czechoslovakia

50352

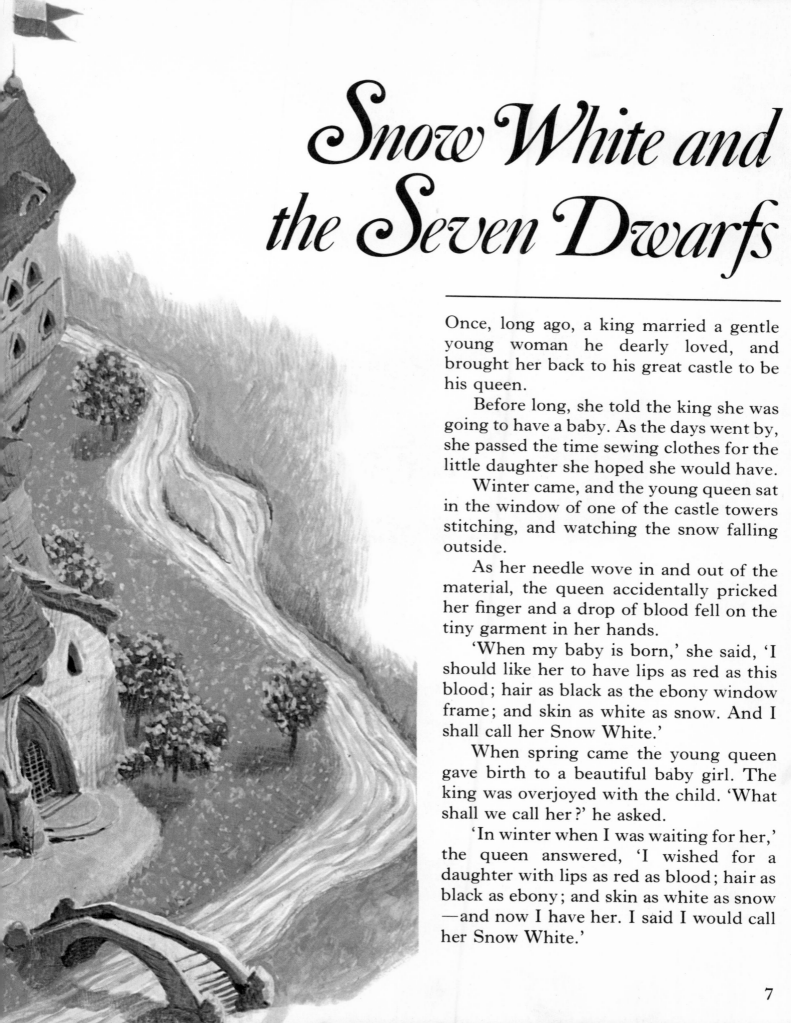

Snow White and the Seven Dwarfs

Once, long ago, a king married a gentle young woman he dearly loved, and brought her back to his great castle to be his queen.

Before long, she told the king she was going to have a baby. As the days went by, she passed the time sewing clothes for the little daughter she hoped she would have.

Winter came, and the young queen sat in the window of one of the castle towers stitching, and watching the snow falling outside.

As her needle wove in and out of the material, the queen accidentally pricked her finger and a drop of blood fell on the tiny garment in her hands.

'When my baby is born,' she said, 'I should like her to have lips as red as this blood; hair as black as the ebony window frame; and skin as white as snow. And I shall call her Snow White.'

When spring came the young queen gave birth to a beautiful baby girl. The king was overjoyed with the child. 'What shall we call her?' he asked.

'In winter when I was waiting for her,' the queen answered, 'I wished for a daughter with lips as red as blood; hair as black as ebony; and skin as white as snow —and now I have her. I said I would call her Snow White.'

7

*'Mirror, mirror in my hand,
Who is the fairest in the land?'*

The king liked this, and to salute the birth had all the flags flown.

Everyone in the castle from the grand duchess to the poorest kitchen-maid loved Snow White. She was always sweet and beautiful from the moment she was born.

Only one person hated the tiny princess, a lady-in-waiting called Perfidia, who had always hoped the king would marry her.

Perfidia always pretended to be fond of Snow White, but really she wished she had never been born. She was eaten up inside with jealousy of her.

Many people in the castle and the town nearby said Perfidia was a witch. They knew she could work magic spells, and that there was a secret room in one of the towers where she used to go to mix mysterious potions.

But Perfidia was polite to the queen and flattering to the king, so they did not realize how wicked she was.

In Lady Perfidia's room was a mirror, and every day she used to hold this up and look at her face in the glass. Then she would say:

'Mirror, mirror, in my hand, who is the fairest in the land?'

And the mirror always replied:

'Fair there be both near and far, but lady you the fairest are.'

And Perfidia used to smile and say to herself, 'I'm even more beautiful than the queen and that baby. The king should have married me, since I'm the fairest.'

But sadly, the young and good queen, who had never been strong, soon died, and Snow White was left in the care of the ladies-in-waiting and the servants in the castle, who were all devoted to her.

As she grew, Snow White played in the grounds guarded by her nurse and the court gardeners. The sentries also kept watch over her.

Sometimes the king himself took her to the top of the tallest tower, up the spiral stone steps, to show her the view—the rivers, forests and mountains which made up his land.

Snow White was left in the care of the ladies-in-waiting and servants.

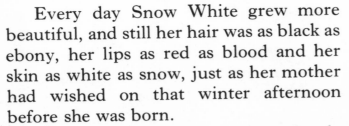

Every day Snow White grew more beautiful, and still her hair was as black as ebony, her lips as red as blood and her skin as white as snow, just as her mother had wished on that winter afternoon before she was born.

In spite of having such a lovely daughter, the king grew lonely, and he married Perfidia, who had been at his side constantly paying him compliments.

So now Perfidia was queen as she had always wished—and Snow White's stepmother. She hated the little girl more than ever whenever she saw her.

The queen flew into a frightful rage.

Each day the new queen used to go to her room and pick up the magic mirror. 'Mirror, mirror, in my hand, who is the fairest in the land?' And the mirror's answer never changed:

'Fair there be both near and far, but queen, of them you the fairest are.'

But the years were passing by, and with every birthday Snow White grew lovelier.

And then one day, the queen asked the usual question and the mirror answered:

'You were the fairest, queen, by far, but Snow White now is fairest star.'

The queen flew into a frightful rage.

10

She looked out of the castle window and saw Snow White standing among the flowers with a fledgling which had fallen out of its nest.

'I don't agree she is fairest,' she said, but all the same she went to her secret room and took out all her face powders and lipsticks and combs and spent three hours making up her face so that it looked like a perfect mask.

Then she returned and asked the mirror the question again.

But it answered as before:

'You were the fairest, queen, by far, but Snow White now is fairest star.'

Something must be done about it, and the baby bird in Snow White's hand gave the wicked queen an idea.

She saw Snow White among the flowers with a fledgling which had fallen out of its nest.

She decided to do something very bad. She sent for a huntsman she knew well to be a strong and cruel man, who did not hesitate to kill a wild boar with his hunting knife, or shoot wild ducks and geese with his arrows.

The queen ordered her servants to go away so that she could be left alone with the huntsman.

When they had gone she lowered her voice and said in a whisper,

'Do you know the Princess Snow White?'

The huntsman answered, 'I've seen her riding by on her white pony when her servants have taken her into the forest for a picnic. I've seen her in her fine carriage and just now, in the garden. Saving yourself, O queen, it's said everywhere that she is growing more beautiful than anyone in the land.'

'Perhaps!' said the queen, her eyes flashing angrily. 'But I don't wish to hear your comments. I have a task for you.'

She leant closer.

'On pain of death if you fail, I order you to take Snow White into the forest, and there you are to kill her. If you succeed, I shall reward you. If you fail, I shall tell the king a story about you that will make him set his soldiers and dogs on you and put you to death.'

The huntsman was a rough and harsh man but he looked at the queen with amazement. He could see that her face was twisted with anger and guessed that she was horribly jealous of Snow White.

He bowed. The queen stood up.

'Follow me to Snow White,' she said.

'On pain of death if you fail,'
said the queen to the huntsman.

Although the huntsman was a hard man, he did not like what the queen was ordering him to do. Yet he had no choice but to obey.

The queen brought him up to Snow White and led the princess to a part of the castle grounds where there were trees. In the wall was a small door, to which she had the key.

'This kind huntsman has come to tell me that he has found a nest of baby black-birds in the forest, and knowing how fond you are of wild creatures, I have asked him to take you to see them. He will take care of you.'

The queen opened the gate and let them out. Snow White took the huntsman by the hand and went with him trustingly. The queen waved good-bye, smiling.

When the king asked where Snow White was the queen told him 'at a picnic', and when the servants wanted to know, she said 'with the king'. So nobody worried.

In the forest Snow White walked along beside the huntsman. He lifted her across the mud where the rain had lain, and untangled brambles from her dress.

Soon they were so far into the forest the tree branches laced overhead made things dark and frightening. Snow White clung to the huntsman tightly.

'I've been ordered by the queen to kill you,' said the huntsman, 'but I'm no murderer. You'll have to get out of the forest as best you can. Probably the wild animals will get you.'

He had been silent all the way but at last looked down at Snow White. His hand felt the handle of his knife, but though he tried to take it from his belt, he could not bring himself to do so. He stopped and turned to her.

'I've been ordered by the queen to kill you—to use this knife on you!'

And now he held it high, but no!

'If I don't kill you she will find someone else who will. And I shall be put to death for my soft heart. But I'm a hunter not a murderer. So I'm going to set you free. You'll have to get out of the forest as best as you can. Probably the wild animals will get you.'

He patted her shoulder and went away back towards the castle. Snow White ran on into the forest. She wanted to get as far away from her wicked stepmother as she could.

She heard many sounds of wild animals—or thought they were. Sometimes she thought she heard a wild boar crashing through the trees; sometimes she thought she could hear the howling of a pack of wolves. But she liked the hedgehogs and rabbits she saw.

The mountains were nearby. Snow White wondered where she could find some food, and where she was going to sleep that night. What was she going to do?

Snow White stopped to drink some water from a stream, and suddenly felt so tired she lay down on the grass and fell fast asleep.

Two ducks found her where she was lying. They lived in the forest and knew everyone in it from the thrushes to the wood-cutters and their dogs.

'Look!' said one, 'A beautiful girl!'

'She must be lost, poor little girl,' said one of the ducks.

'Look at the jewels in her hair and her fine clothes. She must be a princess!' said the other.

'She must be lost. Poor little girl.'

The two ducks stood puzzling what to do next.

'Do you think we should leave her lying there? She looks so tired.'

'Nonsense!' said the duck wearing spectacles. 'The grass will give her a bad chill. We must wake her up and help her. I know where we could take her.' And he whispered in his friend's ear. 'Isn't that a good idea?'

'The best. Wake up, pretty girl. We know you're lost and want to help.'

After a long walk they came to a strange little house made of mushrooms, with a toadstool for a chimney.

When Snow White woke up at last, the first thing she saw was the ducks, bending over her anxiously.

'If you'll come with us,' said the one with the spectacles, 'we'll show you a house where you are sure to be able to stay. The people who own it are very kind.'

They hopped and flew round her and ahead of her, until after a long walk they came to a strange little house made of mushrooms, with a toadstool for a chimney. It had a heavy oak door which was fastened with a large iron bolt.

'This is it,' said the ducks. 'The owners are friends of ours.'

'They must be very small,' said Snow White, looking at the size of the door.

'This is it,' said the ducks. 'The owners are friends of ours.'

Inside there were seven little stools and a low table. The house was so untidy it looked as if no-one had ever cleaned it or put anything away.

'I'm afraid that the owners have to work so hard in the mines all day long that they don't have time to cook or do housework,' apologized the first duck.

'Yes,' said the other, 'they need someone to look after them.'

And they looked hopefully at Snow White.

'I suppose now you're not lost you'll be going home?'

Snow White shook her head and her eyes filled with tears.

'No, I won't be going home,' she said. 'So I'll need somewhere to live. This would be just what I'd like. And if I'm going to take care of your friends, I'd better begin.'

So Snow White and the two ducks set to work. First they swept the ashes out of the fireplace, then they went to the wood outside and collected twigs and logs. Soon a warm fire was blazing.

Next Snow White found some meat in the larder. She went outside with the ducks and together they dug and pulled up carrots and onions and turnips for a stew. Snow White got it ready and hung the pot over the fire to cook.

'If you collect the washing, I'll sweep and dust and make the beds,' she said. And she gave a huge yawn.

Snow White and the two ducks set to work.

The mushroom house belonged to the dwarfs. Every day these quaint little men, who were no higher than Snow White's knee, went out to work in the copper and gold mines under the mountains.

They left the cottage before sunrise, taking their lanterns and picks with them and wearing mushroom and toadstool hats on their heads to protect them in their work.

At the mine they climbed down a long ladder into the underground tunnel and from there went into caves, where they hacked the gold and copper ore from the walls and roof of the cave.

In the evening they marched back home again in a line, singing loudly. They were so tired after working hard all day that they never had time to have more than a rough meal and go straight to bed.

On the day Snow White arrived, the dwarfs came in sight of their house and saw a light in the window and smoke coming from the chimney.

'Look!' cried one. 'There's a light burning. We must have left the lamp alight this morning!'

'But there's smoke coming out of the chimney too,' said another. 'Even if we had left the fire burning it would have gone out by now.'

The dwarfs stood in a little group and stared at their house.

'That's very strange.'

'We'd better go and investigate,' said the boldest and youngest dwarf.

'Don't be silly,' said the oldest dwarf, holding him back. 'You don't know who's in there. It could be robbers who have found our little house and are making themselves comfortable.'

'There aren't any robbers in this part

*In the evening the dwarfs marched
back home in a line, singing loudly.*

of the forest,' scoffed another dwarf.

'Robbers have horses, don't they?
They can travel, can't they? No, you can
be sure that someone has told some bad
men that there is a cosy little house left
empty all day long, and they've come
along to occupy it,' said the oldest.

The dwarfs looked at their mushroom
home with dismay.

'Now, what I suggest we do is this:
I'll creep along to the door and quietly
open it a little way and I'll peep inside,'
said the oldest dwarf.

'Oh, you are brave,' shivered the
others.

'One of us has to do it because we
can't stay out here all night. While I'm
doing this you others keep watch and have
your picks ready in case the people inside
are robbers and rush out at me.'

Keeping their lamps low, the dwarfs

crept up to the house and the oldest dwarf
pushed the door open softly.

'The bolt was undone,' he turned and
whispered to the others. Then he looked
inside.

'Humbles jumbles!' he cried and,
forgetting to be careful, pushed the door
wide open. 'Look!'

They all stepped into the house and
looked round them with amazement.

'Hey!' said the first dwarf. 'Who's
been sitting on my stool?'

'Hey!' said the second dwarf. 'Who's
been laying out my bowl?'

'Hey!' said the third dwarf. 'Who's
been cutting up my bread?'

'Hey!' said the fourth dwarf. 'Who's
been digging up my carrots?'

'Hey!' said the fifth dwarf. 'Who's
been cooking with my fork?'

'Hey!' said the sixth dwarf. 'Who's
been carving meat with my knife?'

'Hey!' said the seventh dwarf. 'Who's
been pouring out my wine?'

Suddenly with a flutter of wings and
quacking with laughter, the ducks came
out from behind the door.

'What do you think of this, then?'
they asked, jumping and hopping with
excitement. 'Don't you think we've done
some good work for you today?'

'It's wonderful!' exclaimed the
dwarfs. 'But why? Why did you do it?'

The table was laid with seven bowls.
There was a delicious smell of stew from
the pot cooking over the fire. Everything
in the room was clean and neat and
shining.

'And to surprise you!' said the ducks...

The dwarfs went over to the stairs
where the ducks were pointing and up to
the room where they slept.

'Who is she,' said the dwarfs. 'How did she get here?'

They crammed through the door and stared. Snow White was lying stretched out across all seven beds, fast asleep.

'Who is she?' asked the dwarfs, 'How did she come here? Why is she asleep?

'She is a beautiful girl,' said the youngest dwarf.'

'And she must be the one who swept

the house,' said the oldest, 'because there's the broom.'

'I should think she's asleep because she got so tired doing all this work,' said one of the other dwarfs.

Just then Snow White stirred and stretched her arms and opened her eyes. She sat up with a start when she saw the strange little men with mushroom hats and long white beards.

At last one asked, 'Who are you and what are you doing here?'

Snow White answered, 'You must be the owners of this dear little house. The kind friends the ducks told me about you.'

The dwarfs smiled shyly.

'I am the king's daughter, Snow White,' she went on, 'and my stepmother, Queen Perfidia, sent me into the forest with a huntsman, who had orders to kill me. But he took pity on me and spared my life. Then these two kind ducks helped me and showed me the way here. They thought I was lost. So here I am. I hope you don't mind.'

'Not at all!' cried the dwarfs all at once. 'But perhaps this house is too poor for a princess to live in.'

'I think it's perfect,' said Snow White.

'Good-bye Sunday, Monday, Tuesday, Wednesday, Thursday, Friday, Saturday.'

'and as I dare not go back to my father's castle in case the queen tries to kill me again, I should be very glad if I could stay here. I could do the housework and cooking for you.'

'That would be wonderful,' said the dwarfs. 'We don't have much time for keeping house after working hard all day in the mines.'

So Snow White came to live with the dwarfs, and she soon found out they were called by the days of the week.

Meanwhile, the huntsman had returned to the castle and had told the queen that Snow White was dead. She rewarded him well, then hurried to the magic mirror.

She gazed into it, smiling, and asked, 'Mirror, mirror in my hand, who is the fairest in the land?' And the mirror answered:

'You fairest in the land have been,
But Snow White in the forest green,
Who with the dwarfs lives far away,
Is fairest in the land today.'
The queen could not believe her ears. So Snow White was not dead!

'I'll kill her yet!' she screamed.

The queen was wild with rage. In her temper she knocked over the mirror and

'I'll kill her yet!' screamed the queen.

27

broke a precious jar and plate. Then she sent for the huntsman, but he had wisely left for the forest.

When the servants could not find him the queen hurried away to her secret room and took out a book of spells and potions. For Queen Perfidia was indeed a witch, as everyone had always suspected.

'I shall not rest until Snow White is dead and I am again the fairest in the land,' she said to herself.

She collected a basket of colourful and strong ribbons and laces. Then she disguised herself as an old woman and set off to find Snow White.

The ducks pulled the ends of the ribbons.

Nobody at the castle noticed her slip away, because the alarm was out that Snow White was missing and everyone was searching for her.

The queen had a tame bird which flew ahead and showed her the way to the dwarfs' house in the forest near the mountains.

On this day the dwarfs had gone to the mine as usual. They never dreamed that the queen could have discovered that Snow White was still alive, and even less that she knew where she was living.

Only the ducks were suspicious when the old woman came hobbling along the path to where Snow White was picking flowers. They flapped about to warn Snow White, but she had such a kind nature that she did not think this poor old woman could mean her any harm.

'Would you like to buy some ribbons and help a poor old beggar-woman, my dear?'

'Why yes, they're very pretty,' said Snow White, choosing four of the brightest colours.

'Let me tie them round your dress,' said the old woman. She drew the ribbons so tightly round Snow White's waist that the girl could not breathe and fell down senseless on the grass.

If it had not been for the ducks, Snow White might have died. After the queen had gone they pulled the ends of the ribbons and loosened them until Snow White could breathe again.

At the castle the king and all the courtiers and servants were grieving and weeping, because they were beginning to think Snow White might be dead.

Queen Perfidia pretended to cry too, but she couldn't wait to get to the mirror, and ask the question:

'Mirror, mirror, in my hand,
Who is the fairest in the land?'
And to her fury the mirror answered:
'You fairest in the land have been,
But Snow White in the forest green,
Who with the dwarfs lives far away,
Is fairest in the land today.'

'This time I shall make certain,' she swore. She dipped the teeth of a pretty comb in strong poison, then put the comb in a tray of beads and bracelets.

She disguised herself as a middle-aged

pedlar-woman and once again set out for the forest.

The dwarfs were worried when they were told what had happened to Snow White.

'On no account go outside when a stranger is around,' they told her.

She promised faithfully that she would stay indoors, and they went off to work.

Soon the queen came along the path and knocked on the door of the dwarfs' house.

'Would you like to buy a pretty comb?' she said when Snow White opened the door.

She looked so different from the old beggar-woman that Snow White was completely deceived.

'Try this one,' said the queen, holding up the poisoned comb. 'No need to buy it if it isn't right.'

As soon as Snow White drew the comb through her hair she fell down unconscious on the floor. Chuckling happily, the queen hurried back to the castle.

Fortunately, one of the dwarfs had come up out of the mine that morning for some fresh air. He noticed the queen's tame bird flying in the direction of their house with a comb in his beak.

He told the others and they thought the queen might be up to something, so they put down their tools and hurried back home. They were not in time to catch the queen, but they found Snow White in time.

'Look!' said Tuesday, and pulled the comb out from Snow White's hair. As soon as he did this the poison stopped working, and she opened her eyes.

This time the queen was sure the mirror would give the right answer:

'Mirror, mirror, in my hand,
Who is the fairest in the land?'
And the mirror answered:
'You fairest in the land have been,
But Snow White in the forest green,
Who with the dwarfs lives far away,
Is fairest in the land today.'
'I can't have made the poison strong enough,' raged the queen. 'And I should have made her swallow it.'

She sent a servant to the gardener for a basket of his finest apples. Then she got to work with her poison recipes.

She injected a large amount of deadly poison into the red side of one apple. Then she changed herself into a gypsy.

*'I can't have made the poison strong
enough!' raged the queen.*

Next day, before the dwarfs set off to work, they spoke to Snow White.

'Dearest Snow White, we love you very much and since you have come to live with us we have been happier and more comfortable than in all our days . . . and you know that dwarfs usually live to be many years old. So you are precious.

'Now we've discovered a new place in our mine which is full of rare and precious stones—diamonds, rubies, emeralds, sapphires—and we have a lot of work to do. But we won't be able to get our work done if we're worrying about you falling into the wicked queen's trap.'

Snow White nodded and kissed them.

'I understand, Sunday, Monday, Tuesday, Wednesday, Thursday, Friday, Saturday, and I promise to be more careful from now on.'

'Remember the queen knows magic and can wear many disguises. Do not go out, and do not open the door to anyone while we are gone.'

'I promise,' said Snow White. 'Trust me. I will be really careful and if anything happens I'll send the ducks to tell you at once.'

So the dwarfs went off to their new mine and worked busily all day.

'We've discovered a new place in our mine which is full of rare and precious stones— diamonds, emeralds, rubies and sapphires . . .'

33

This time the queen had not only put on a disguise and painted her face so it looked different.

She had also swallowed a magic potion which totally changed her features and made her look much younger.

She came along the forest path with the basket of apples on her arm, singing and looking just like a gypsy girl. When she went by the dwarfs' house she stopped and waved to Snow White, who was looking out of the window.

'Buy some of my apples,' cried the gypsy with a smile as she held up the poisonous one.

Snow White looked at her for a long time. No—this could not be the queen. Her face was entirely different. But she kept her promise to the dwarfs and just opened the window.

'They're very good apples,' said the queen. 'Try this one. Look, I'll take a bite to prove it is a good apple.'

And she took a big bite from the green side, and munched it. Nothing happened to her. Snow White hesitated. She wanted very much to buy some of the apples for the dwarfs as they were difficult to come by deep in the forest.

The ducks became anxious and flew about quacking and beating their wings near Snow White.

'It's all right,' she whispered. 'I'm quite sure she isn't the queen. I know my stepmother well and the gypsy is not anything like her.'

And Snow White let her into the house.

'Buy some of my lovely apples,' said the gypsy to Snow White.

'Here, try the red side. It's the best and I've left it for you to taste.'

Snow White took a bite as the gypsy girl suggested. As soon as the piece of apple was in Snow White's mouth, the poison made her fall down as if dead.

The wicked queen listened to her heart, and watch to see if she was still breathing.

'Yes, she's dead this time,' laughed the queen, and she hurried away.

Snow White lay pale and still, her eyes closed. The two ducks flapped and squawked and fanned her with their wings. But she did not stir.

One of them flew to find the dwarfs at the mine, while the other stayed to look after Snow White. He went on trying to wake her up, but it was no good.

Snow White lay pale and still, her eyes closed.

When they heard the news, the dwarfs hurried back with the duck. They looked at their dear Snow White, so white and not breathing, and knew that this time the wicked queen had succeeded. Nothing they tried would revive her.

'That wicked, evil queen,' they sobbed. 'How could she be so cruel to our kind, beautiful Snow White?'

But at the castle, the queen dressed in her finest clothes and jewels was dancing at a great ball to celebrate. She was filled with joy, because this time when she had asked the mirror:

'Mirror, mirror, in my hand,
Who is the fairest in the land?'
It had answered:
'Snow White in the forest green,
Was fairest in the land O Queen.
But now that fair Snow White is dead,
You, Queen, the fairest must be said.'

Snow White looked so beautiful where she lay that she did not look dead at all. Her lips were still as red as blood; her hair was still as black as ebony; and her skin was still as white as snow.

The dwarfs could not bear to bury her so they made her a glass coffin and laid her in it on a pillow of flowers.

They put it in the forest for all the wild birds and animals to see, and every day they came to see her and bring bunches of fresh flowers.

The two ducks stayed close to her too. Everyone loved Snow White and couldn't bear to be parted from her.

It happened that one day two servants of a prince were riding by, and they saw the strange scene of the dwarfs gathered round the glass coffin. They could see a lovely young girl in it who seemed to be asleep.

'Look!' they said, 'Isn't she beautiful? Wouldn't the prince be interested to hear about this?'

The white-haired servant said, 'I think we ought to ride back and tell him at once. He might want to see her.'

*'I think we ought to ride back
and tell the prince at once,' said
the white-haired servant.*

The two servants rode back to the
castle where their master lived. They told
him about the dwarfs they had come
across standing round a glass coffin with
the most beautiful girl they had ever seen
lying in it.

'And where did you say this was?'
asked the prince.

'I must go there at once. Perhaps I may
be able to do something to help,' said the
prince.

He called for his cloak and his hat, and

he ran down to the stable where his horse was being saddled.

The prince jumped on and galloped off in the direction of the mountains and the forest. The two servants could hardly keep up with him.

'Is this the way?' the prince would shout back over his shoulder.

'Yes sire, straight along the forest track,' they would shout back, panting.

When they reached the place in the forest where Snow White was lying the prince jumped down from his horse, walked to the glass coffin and gazed down at Snow White.

'She's the most beautiful maiden I've ever set eyes on,' he said. 'But she doesn't look really dead. Only asleep. Let us lift her out of the coffin and see if she is indeed dead.'

When he and the two servants, helped by the dwarfs, gently lifted the coffin down, one of the servants tripped over a tree root. It gave the coffin a sharp jolt.

The movement jerked the piece of poisoned apple which was stuck in Snow White's throat, and made her cough. She spluttered and spat out the apple and opened her eyes.

Strong as the poison was, Snow White had not been killed because she had not actually swallowed it.

The prince was handsome, young and rich, and he had been looking for a bride for many months. But whenever he was introduced to a suitable princess, he said afterwards, 'She is beautiful but she's boring,' or, 'She's interesting but much too ugly.'

The king and queen, his parents, were beginning to despair that their unruly son would never marry and settle down.

But as soon as he saw Snow White he fell in love with her, and swore that he would never marry anyone else. And when she saw him, she fell in love too.

Snow White spluttered and then opened her eyes. The prince said she was the most beautiful maiden he had ever set eyes on.

The prince carried Snow White back to his castle on his horse, where they were married amidst great rejoicing.

On the day of their wedding, Queen Perfidia picked up her mirror and said,
    'Mirror, mirror, in my hand,
    'Who is the fairest in the land?'
And to her horror the mirror replied:
    'You were the fairest by far, O Queen,
    But the prince's bride serene,
    Snow White now is the fairest seen.'
The queen choked and dropped dead from the shock. And Snow White and the prince lived happily ever after.

The prince carried Snow White back to the castle on his horse.

The Lion and the Joiner

Have you ever thought how strange it is that animals allow human beings to rule over them? Even those animals who are twice as large as the people and have much more savage teeth and claws?

It is true that in the jungle men have to be cunning when some of the more fierce wild animals are around, but they generally manage to avoid being harmed and often succeed in trapping them alive.

You would imagine, for instance, that a cow would know that she is large enough with those horns to turn on the farmer driving her along the lane and say 'Shan't!' but not a bit of it.

A child can sometimes herd several cows from the meadow to be milked, and when he shouts 'Get a move on!' the cows lumber along obediently.

Tigers and lions are more difficult to manage, but if they are not careful they can end up in cages too.

It is all a matter of who is the cleverest . . . man or the animals.

There was once a young lion who had never before met a human in his life, who thought he could deal with a poor joiner (another name for a carpenter) who came along quite easily.

But see what happened when he tried to tell the joiner what to do.

It began on an island far away in the deep blue ocean. No human being had ever set foot on this peaceful place, and all the animals and birds and other creatures lived there in peaceful friendship.

On this island grew exotic flowers and many other strange and lovely plants. Silver streams rustled through tall grass and rushes and at the edge of the water lived hundreds of water birds and frogs, and thousands of insects, including glow-worms.

Two stately swans had a nest on one side of a willow tree, and on the other side lived a duck.

This duck was not brave, but she did not mind flying over the wood where apes and monkeys lived, or landing among the herds of zebra and antelope on the plain. She was not afraid, at a distance, of lions and tigers.

But the duck was afraid of human beings, though she had never seen one.

A bird who had travelled to far off countries where men and women lived once told the duck that even the largest animals were not safe from man. They could hunt and trap elephants and seals and harpoon the giant whales.

As for ducks, this bird told her friend that that when ducks got near men they were usually caught for supper. This gave the duck dreadful nightmares.

The duck turned round and saw a young
lion with a friendly face.

*'I had a fearful dream,' the little
duck told the lion.*

strange land. At once she heard a voice
say, 'Duck, this is a country where men
live. Do not rest here on your flight.' It
was the dream voice again.

The duck squawked with fright, and
suddenly she realized there was someone
behind her. She turned round and saw a
young lion with a friendly face.

'What frightens you, little duck?'
he asked her. 'Where do you come from?'

'I'm a duck from an island three days
and three nights flight away from here,'
answered the duck timidly.

'And why have you come here?' asked
the lion curiously.

'I had a fearful dream,' the little duck
told him. 'And a voice told me that man is
dangerous and warned me to leave my
home and fly away to escape him. I've just
heard it again.'

'I too have had a dream like that,' said
the young lion. 'It made me think of my
father's warning that I should always
beware man.'

The lion and the duck stayed in each
other's company and even slept beside
each other for some time.

*The lion and the duck slept beside each
other for some time.*

49

They were woken up by a clatter of hooves. They rose up to see what was coming towards them in the cloud of dust they could see on the road.

The hooves stopped close to them and the dust slowly cleared. There stood a donkey which squealed with fright when it saw the lion and bucked its hind legs and brayed, *EEEEEoooor . . . EEEEEooor*!

The duck fluttered up and descended before she realized there was no danger from this poor old donkey with a broken tethering rope trailing down.

The lion said to the donkey, 'Listen you, donkey, what made you come running towards us like that? And so noisy?'

The donkey answered bowing to the lion, 'O son of the king of the animals, I'm running away from man.'

'What!' asked the lion cub. 'Are you afraid that he'll kill you?'

'No, not kill me,' the donkey replied, 'but I fear him because he tries to put a halter on my head. This man has a thing called a saddle which he fixes on my back and I have to carry huge loads of hay or bales of cloth. And he has a thing called girths which he straps round my body.

'He has another thing called a crupper which he puts under my tail. And worst of all, he has a stick called a goad with which he prods me and whacks me. And he rides on me. This man makes me work so hard for him I almost collapse and fall down with exhaustion.'

The donkey paused while the lion listened, nodding. The duck felt more and more how terrible man must be. She could not think what this terrifying being called man must look like.

'And when I grow old and can no longer work for him,' the donkey went on,

There stood a donkey which squealed with fright when it saw the lion.

'the man will deliver me to the water-carriers who will load my back with flagons full of water from the river. My life will get worse and worse in this way every day till I die.'

And the donkey groaned, *EEEEEoo-oor, EEEEEoooor*.

'So when I had a chance I broke this rope which was tied to the gatepost and ran away as fast as my legs would go.'

The duck felt her feathers ruffling up and her skin creeping over with goose-pimples when she heard the story.

'Perhaps, sir and madam, you could tell me where I could run to hide from this man who tries me so,' he said.

'What a miserable creature you are!' said the young lion, 'to be afraid of a being smaller than yourself. Why don't you turn and face him? You won't catch me being frightened of a man.'

While the lion, the duck and the donkey were talking, they saw far away another cloud of dust rolling towards them. A loud clattering of hooves sounded, and it stopped near them.

The cloud of dust lifted and there stood a fine black stallion with a waving mane and tail, pawing the earth and tossing its head and snorting.

When the horse saw the three of them he neighed and pawed the air, kicking up with his hind legs.

The young lion was amazed by this magnificent animal. He had never seen a horse before, and he said:

'What kind of animal are you? And why are you galloping to the desert with such terror?'

The horse replied, 'O son of the king of the animals, I'm a horse, and I'm running away from my master, man.'

The lion was shocked and said to him, 'Don't speak in that way. Shame on you. You're proud and large and strong. How can you run away from a creature who is smaller and weaker than you?'

The horse laughed.

'Don't let my size and strength fool

When the horse saw the three of them he neighed and pawed the air, kicking up with his hind legs.

you. This man who is my master is so cunning he can tie my legs together with a thing called a hobble so I can neither sit nor lie down. If he wants to ride on my back he puts a saddle on me and sits upon it with his feet in iron hoops.

'He puts a piece of iron in my mouth called a bit, and ties a thong of leather to it called a rein.

'What kind of animal are you?' asked the lion.

'Then he makes me go for him by guiding me with those reins, and by hitting me with his whip. And when I'm old I shall be sold to the knacker for horsemeat. So I've run away.'

53

While the lion cub, the duck and the horse and the donkey were talking, there rose yet another cloud of dust, and when it cleared they saw a camel.

When the lion saw how big and awful this creature was with his long legs and humps, he thought here at last must be a man. He roared and was just about to spring at him and tear him apart with his strong teeth when the others stopped him.

The lion thought that here at last he saw a man.

The horse said 'This is not man, O son of the king of the animals. This is a camel.'

The camel lumbered over and bowed.

'You worthless object,' said the lion. 'Are you going to tell me that with your huge bones and tall legs, so suited to kick with, you are afraid of this creature man like these others here?'

The camel said, 'O princely lion, have you not heard of the cleverness of man? He can think of ways of taming beasts as huge as me that nobody would guess.

'He puts a thing in my nose called a nose-ring, and then he ties a rope to it, and the smallest of his little children can lead me by it.

'This man, my master, piles my humps with heavy loads and makes me carry them on long journeys. And like the horse, I too when I am old will go to the knacker who gets rid of me—skin and bones, teeth and all.'

'When did you last see this creature?' asked the lion.

'At sunset,' said the camel. 'I've run away and he'll be coming to find me.'

'Then I'll go and find him,' the lion said, 'and I shall deal with him with my claws and my roar and my teeth.'

'Then I shall go and find him,'
said the lion.

Not long after they had set out they saw in the distance coming towards them a little thin creature with skinny, crooked legs and a crooked back.

As he came closer they could see he carried a tool-box on his arm and a pile of planks on his head.

'I shall protect you,' said the lion.

The animals stood watching him coming anxiously—except for the duck, who flew up into the branch of a tree, and the lion, who stood looking at him boldly.

'Is that a man?' asked the lion in disbelief.

'Yes,' whispered the others trembling.

'The creature you're all so afraid of?'

'Take care,' quacked the duck. 'Recall the warning the king your father gave you about men. Be cautious of him.'

The joiner came up to the animals and looked from one to the other and bowed.

The young lion said to him, 'What are you doing here?'

The man bowed again politely and said, 'O, brave proud lion, I have come to ask for your help. I am a joiner, that is a sort of carpenter, and I'm running away from my master.'

The young lion glanced back at the other animals, who were listening with very suspicious looks on their faces. Then he held up his paw.

'I shall protect you,' he said, 'and you needn't be afraid any longer. I have sharp claws and fearful teeth and strong sinews and a mighty roar, so I shall look after you.'

'A thousand thanks, O son of the king of the animals,' said the carpenter, bowing and scraping. 'You've saved me. You're my noble rescuer.

'This man who is my master,' said the joiner, 'has always treated me badly. He has kept me running to do his work from morning till night, and never gave me enough to eat, so you can see how weak it has made me. He paid me only poor wages so that my wife and little children had a hard time too. So I have become ill.' And the man sighed.

The young lion looked over the thin joiner and roared with anger.

'This really is a scandal,' he cried. 'I shall show that man my claws. But Mr Joiner, where are you going with that stack of wood? Surely it is much too heavy for such a small and hungry creature as you to carry?'

The joiner set the pile of planks on the ground and wiped the drops of perspiration from his forehead.

'You are right, young lion. They are too heavy for me. But I haven't got much further to go with them. To tell you what I'm doing, as it might interest you, it concerns a relation of yours. I'm on my way to your uncle, the leopard.'

'The leopard!' exclaimed the young lion. 'My own uncle?'

'The very same,' said the joiner, giving him a sly look. 'He has asked me to come and build him a hut—a strong wooden hut with a door. That's where I'm carrying these planks and this hammer and nails.'

'What!' the young lion roared, his voice full of jealousy, 'you're going to build a house for my uncle the leopard! Let him build a house for himself! My father is the king of the animals and as I am son of the king, I think my wishes should come first.'

'Why, do you want a hut for yourself, sir?' asked the joiner with a further cunning look at the lion.

'I certainly do,' said the cub angrily, though he had not thought of having one until this moment.

'Respectfully, sir,' said the joiner, 'I shall make your hut immediately after I have finished building the hut for your uncle.'

The spindly man bowed and his crooked bones creaked, and he went on very, very politely, 'But I feel that I cannot begin any other work until I have carried out this job I said I would do for your uncle the leopard. When I give my word, then that is a promise. If I broke my promise, then grand people like your uncle wouldn't ask me to work for them any more.'

'Grand people like my uncle!' said the young lion bristling. 'Why, he has to take second place to the king, and to the king's son I'll have you know!'

'Granted, O son of the king of the animals,' said the joiner touching his hat in a way that showed the other animals that he was making fun of the lion cub. 'And I'll tell you what, highness, as soon as I've finished the hut for the leopard I'll start on the one for you. That's fair, isn't it?'

'No, it isn't fair,' exclaimed the cub, 'And I insist on you doing mine first.'

'The truth is, sir,' said the joiner, 'that I'm afraid of your uncle's huge claws and terrible muscles and sinews that could tear me up in little bits for his breakfast, if I annoy him and don't do the work in time.'

'The carpenter is going to play a trick on the young cub,' whispered the camel to the horse.

The duck flew down flapping her wings and squawking loudly, 'Take care, take care, remember the king's warning. Beware of men and their cunning ways.'

But the lion was in a temper now.

'So!' he said to the joiner. 'You are afraid of his claws. Well have a feel of

'I'm on my way to your uncle, the leopard,' said the joiner.

The young lion pressed his claws into the joiner's chest.

mine,' and he let fly, roaring.

He leapt at the joiner with a mighty growl and gave him such a push that he fell over.

The young lion pressed his claws into the joiner's chest and frightened him by showing him his strong sinews stretched over him.

The animals and birds watching were afraid for a moment that the lion was going to kill the carpenter, but they still suspected that somehow the man was going to get the better of their friend.

'Very well, sir,' said the joiner, getting up rather shakily and dusting his clothes. 'If you insist, I will make you a hut first, and go to your uncle the leopard next.'

And he gave another cunning look and searched in his tool-box for a measuring rule.

'Be so good as to stand there, sir, please,' said the joiner, and he laid the measure along the lion's back with a flourish and a wink.

'What's that for?' asked the cub.

'Just to get your size so the hut will fit you, highness,' said the man with a bow. The watchers felt more and more nervous. What was the man up to?

The carpenter sawed up the planks to the measurements he had taken from the lion, and began to hammer them together. First he made a base and then four sides, but he left the top open.

'If you'd just step in and try your hut for size,' said the joiner.

The lion climbed into the box. 'It's too small,' he growled. 'I can't turn round.'

'I'll adjust it,' said the man, and he nailed some planks on top.

The young lion was trapped.

'Let me out! Let me out!' he roared,

The lion climbed into the box. 'It's too small,' he growled. 'I can't turn round.'

The joiner nailed some planks on top.

'Let me out!' roared the lion.

The duck and the camel and the horse and the donkey watched sadly. The joiner had tricked the lion completely.

and he rattled about inside the box so hard he might have shaken it to pieces. But the joiner had made it strong and the lion couldn't escape.

'Go to sleep, young lion,' laughed the carpenter. 'I thought that you could easily overcome a skinny little poor old man like me with your claws and sinews.'

'I'll tear you into shreds,' raged the lion cub. 'You can't keep me here.' The lion banged and rattled and roared but he could do nothing about it. The joiner had tricked him completely.

'Ho! Ho!' laughed the joiner, 'Ha! Ha! I may not be so very young and strong, and I may not roar and have claws, but I'm certainly better at some things.'

He patted the box cheerfully. 'I shall feed my family for a week on what I'm paid for you by the circus.

The duck and the camel and the horse and the donkey watched sadly.

'If only he had listened to the dream. He was warned,' said the duck. 'Even his father the king of the animals said be cautious of men. I think I'll fly back to my old island after all.'

Abdullah from the Land and Abdullah from the Sea

Once upon a time there was a fisherman called Abdullah. Every day he left his home near the sea and went to catch fish.

He had fine strong nets with corks round the edges which he used to cast out in the water, and nearly every day when he hauled them in there would be a catch of shimmering silver fish in them.

Up till now Abdullah had always managed to catch enough fish to feed his family, and a small amount over to sell in the market. And as he had nine children he relied on his luck every day. If he didn't come home with the fish, the family wouldn't have any supper.

But his children were healthy and happy and Abdullah and his wife had a good life even if they were poor.

They never thought it would ever be any different, and would never have dreamed that one day they would live in the sultan's palace, and that their son would marry the sultan's daughter.

It began quite differently with bad luck, not good luck. One day Abdullah went down to the sea as usual for his day's fishing. The sky looked heavy and threatening and the sea was dark and strange instead of its usual sunny blue.

Abdullah cast his nets and waited, and then hauled them in . . . and they were completely empty! Not even a sprat or a minnow in the corner.

He couldn't believe it at first. It had never happened before. So he tried again. Carefully he cast the nets and waited, but still he had no luck. He tried a third time. The net felt extra heavy this time but when Abdullah pulled it in he rubbed his eyes. It was filled only with sand and shells and pebbles.

What sea monster was doing this to him? What had he done to deserve a punishment like this? He tipped out the shells and sand and took up a new position on a rock well out in the water.

Once he thought he saw a flash of some strange creature in the water. It could have been a large fish such as a shark, or even a dolphin, but for a moment it seemed to have a man's head and arms and a beard.

'Perhaps I have angered the god of the sea in some way,' said Abdullah as he pulled up his nets empty for the tenth time, 'though I don't know how.'

In the end he gave up and packed up his nets. As he went home along the shore

'But Abdullah, what shall we have to eat for supper?'

his friends the other fishermen waved to him.

'Good fishing today, Abdullah,' they called out as they tipped out a heap of shimmering fish into their jars.

'Not for me,' he muttered worried.

All the family stared when they saw Abdullah, who was always so jolly, come in with his head bowed. In his house everyone used to gather round the table when he tipped out the fish, but today his basket

'Why Abdullah, what's the matter?' asked the baker.

was completely empty.

He told his wife what had happened and the children listened with round eyes.

'But Abdullah, what shall we have to eat for supper? There isn't any money.'

'I'll just have to go back to the sea tonight and try again by moonlight,' said Abdullah, 'and keep on fishing till I do have a catch.'

He was walking along towards the sea carrying his fishing tackle when his good friend the baker came over to him.

'Why Abdullah, what's the matter?' he asked the fisherman. 'You look very worried. I hope nothing has gone wrong

at home. And why are you going out fishing at this time of night?'

'It's because of the fish,' said Abdullah. 'I have been in my usual place on the sea shore, casting out my nets since before sunrise, and the only thing I caught was sand!'

The baker was astonished.

'I haven't heard any of the other fishermen complaining. I wonder what the reason can be?'

'I don't know,' said Abdullah miserably, 'but I do know we haven't got any food to eat tonight, and I haven't got anything to sell in the market.'

*Abdullah was so grateful
he did not know how to thank the baker.*

'But of course you must have some bread from me. I'll let you have the loaves as usual and you can pay me later when you catch the fish again.'

'That would be great kindness, baker.'

Thanks to the good-hearted baker, the children of Abdullah and his wife had something to eat that night. He went on fishing with only a few hours sleep. But again he hauled up his nets empty. After trying all the next day in vain, Abdullah gave up fishing and wandered home.

As he wandered past the baker's shop he smelt the delicious bread baking, but he could not afford to buy any.

The baker hurried out to speak to him.

'How did it go today, Abdullah?'

'Still no luck I'm afraid, my friend,' said Abdullah. 'I'm sorry, but I'm afraid I shan't be able to pay you for the bread you gave me yesterday.'

'Don't worry about that,' said the baker, pushing several loaves into his hands. 'You can have all the bread you need every day to feed your family, and when things are better, then you can pay me what you owe.'

Abdullah was so grateful he did not know how to thank the kind baker.

Then one day, after forty days, he was sitting on a rock when suddenly he felt his nets pulling heavily. It wriggled and

There in his net was this strange creature, half man with a fish's tail.

73

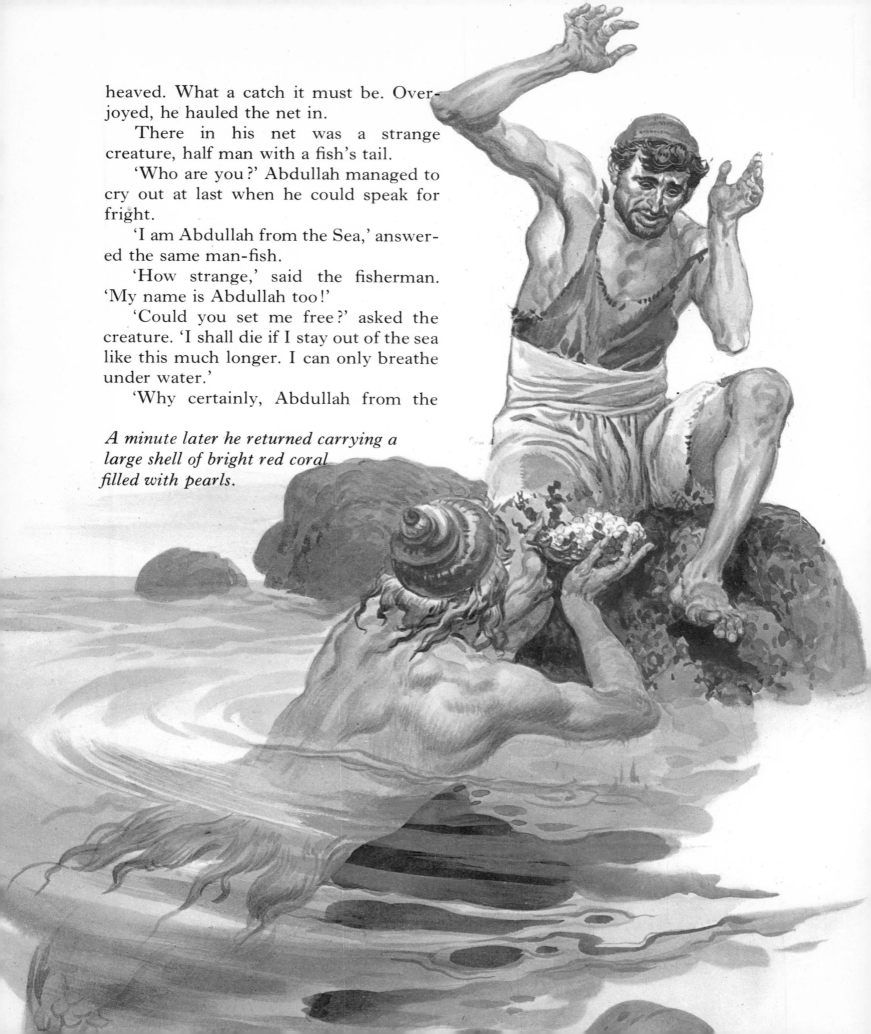

heaved. What a catch it must be. Overjoyed, he hauled the net in.

There in his net was a strange
creature, half man with a fish's tail.

'Who are you?' Abdullah managed to
cry out at last when he could speak for
fright.

'I am Abdullah from the Sea,' answered the same man-fish.

'How strange,' said the fisherman.
'My name is Abdullah too!'

'Could you set me free?' asked the
creature. 'I shall die if I stay out of the sea
like this much longer. I can only breathe
under water.'

'Why certainly, Abdullah from the

*A minute later he returned carrying a
large shell of bright red coral
filled with pearls.*

Sea,' said the fisherman, and helped to disentangle the man-fish from his net.

'Thank you, Abdullah from the Land,' he said and dived away under the water.

A minute later he returned carrying a large shell of bright red coral full to over-flowing with shining pearls, which he gave to the fisherman.

Abdullah's mouth fell open as he took them. The man-fish waved good-bye and dived into the sea and vanished with a flash of his scaly tail.

Carrying the shell full of pearls, Abdullah hurried home.

75

'By the beard of the sultan! What have you got there?' cried the baker.

'Thank you,' Abdullah called after him, but only the waved lapped an answer.

Carrying the shell full of pearls, Abdullah hurried home.

On the way back to town Abdullah said to himself, 'I shall have to take these pearls to a merchant who knows all about such things, and ask him to value them. But first I must go and see my friend the baker and pay him back.'

In the baker's shop Abdullah poured the pearls from the shell on to the counter.

'By the beard of the sultan, what have you got there?' cried the baker.

Abdullah told his friend all about the man-fish and what had happened.

'Half of these are for you,' said Abdullah. 'If it hadn't been for your kindness my family would have starved.'

'But this is too much! I can't have all of these pearls!' said the baker.

'But you must,' said Abdullah. 'You have been generous to me—and not just for a week but for forty days and nights. You never knew when you would be paid. Now it is my turn to be generous.'

He picked up the rest of the pearls and put them in the shell, then paused.

'Could you perhaps let me have some small change for this pearl?' he asked, handing one over. 'To buy something.'

That night Abdullah surprised his friends and neighbours by giving a huge feast. They were amazed when they saw the table loaded with meat and fish, tarts and fruit and nuts, with wine.

The baker made a spiced cake and many sweet things.

'What happened?' everyone asked. 'Yesterday poor, today rich, but how?'

Abdullah kept his secret.

The following morning Abdullah went to market and filled a basket with the finest fruit he could buy. With the basket under his arm he returned to the rock where the day before he had caught the man-fish, and waded up to his waist into

'Abdullah from the Sea, Abdullah come to me . . .'

the sea. He shouted loudly:
    'Abdullah from the Sea,
    Abdullah come to me;
    Abdullah from the Land
    Brings gifts within his hand.
    You gave pearls to me,
    Abdullah from the Sea,
    I bring you fruit to eat,
    It's you I come to greet.'

A moment later the sea whipped up like a whirlpool and there was Abdullah from the Sea.

The man-fish took the basket of fruit smiling with excitement.

'These are for me? Many thanks. We

*The basket was loaded
with hundreds of
magnificent pearls.*

never see fruit under the water in my country. But don't go away. Wait there for me until I come back.'

Abdullah waited, wondering what the man-fish was going to do. After some time, Abdullah from the Sea rose again above the water, holding the fruit basket over his head with both hands.

Instead of peaches and grapes, it was loaded with hundreds of magnificent pearls. Abdullah from the Sea gave them to the fisherman. They were so heavy he could hardly lift them.

He thanked the man-fish over and over

again, then waved good-bye as he dived out of sight. Abdullah dragged the basket, hardly believing his luck.

That day he took some of the pearls to a merchant, who opened his eyes wide when he saw what the poor ragged fisherman had brought to him.

'Have you any more like these?' he

'Have you any more pearls like these?' asked the merchant.

asked, inspecting a huge pearl between his finger and thumb.

'I have a basketful,' said Abdullah.

Whereupon the merchant jumped up and ran out of his shop shouting, 'Stop him! Stop him! He's a thief!'

Before Abdullah could give him a word of explanation, the merchant had called his servants and with their help bound Abdullah with a rope and dragged him through the streets to the palace of the sultan.

When the people in the town saw the scene, they came running up.

'What's he done?' they asked.

'Only stolen the pearls belonging to the sultan's wife!' said the merchant. 'He came and tried to sell them to me. Look, here's one of them!'

And he felt in his pocket and held up one of the pearls he had taken from Abdullah.

'You've heard the sultan's wife lost her pearl necklace. Well, I've found the thief and I'm taking him to the palace and to the sultan himself.'

The people of the town were so angry when they heard this, that they followed

'I've found the thief and I'm taking him to the palace of the sultan,' said the merchant.

Abdullah shouting at him and beating him with their sticks.

Soon the merchant and Abdullah were standing before the sultan.

'What's all this fuss about?' asked the sultan. 'Who is the prisoner?'

The merchant bowed and said proudly, 'Sire, here is the thief.'

'What thief? What has he stolen?' asked the sultan very much astonished.

'Why, the pearls belonging to your wife, sire. They were taken from her not long ago, and this fisherman came to try to sell them to me.'

'What's all this fuss about?' asked the sultan.

The merchant handed the sultan one of the pearls Abdullah had brought him.

The sultan examined the wonderful pearl with amazement and then the rest which had been brought to him in one of the merchant's gold trays.

'I think these pearls are quite out of the ordinary,' he remarked.

'I thought so too,' said the merchant. 'That's why I thought at once of your wife's necklace. I was sure they could not belong to this ragged fellow.'

The sultan sent for his wife, and after a time she appeared.

'You wanted to speak to me, my dear husband?' she asked.

'Yes. Look at these pearls. Are they the ones from your missing necklace?'

The sultan's wife looked at the pearls mystified.

'I think these pearls are quite out of the ordinary.'

'Arrest this dishonest creature,' said the sultan. 'Put him in jail for two days.'

'They can't be, because my necklace has been found.'

'So tell us where you got them from,' said the sultan to the fisherman.

At last Abdullah was able to tell his story. Everyone listened intently.

The sultan nodded and turned to the merchant, who was cringing humbly.

'So you falsely accused this honest man? I won't allow that in my country.

Abdullah was so popular with everyone at the palace that he was made a grand vizier.

Arrest this dishonest creature, guards. Put him in jail for two days.'

The sultan turned to Abdullah. 'Where will you go now, good fisherman? Now you're a rich man?'

Abdullah bowed and said respectfully, 'I shall go back to my home, sire.'

The sultan shook his head in disbelief. 'With so much wealth,' he said, pointing to the pearls, 'you can't live there. It would not be safe. You had better bring your family to stay in my palace. We have vaults here where valuable treasures can be stored. Now everyone knows you possess such precious pearls you would be robbed straight away.'

So Abdullah and his family went to live in the sultan's palace, and the energetic and jolly fisherman was so popular with everyone—the sultan said he was the most sensible man in the palace—that soon he was named grand vizier.

Abdullah did not overlook his kind friend the baker. He arranged for the sultan to try some of his delicious bread. The sultan and his family thought it was the best they had ever tasted, so the baker was appointed to bake always for the court.

As time passed, Abdullah's children began to grow up into handsome and beautiful young men and women. His eldest son fell in love with the daughter of the sultan, and everyone was pleased. Abdullah gave them many pearls for a wedding present. And this reminded him of the man-fish.

His eldest son fell in love with the daughter of the sultan.

'It's too long since I visited the sea and gave some fruit to my friend,' thought Abdullah. Although he never on any day forgot that he owed his good fortune to the strange man-fish.

Since Abdullah had become grand vizier he could not get to the sea as often as he wished, but he liked to have his house near, now he had his own home.

Whenever he had a chance and could walk on the shore, he would think of the days when he was poor, and his family had to wear patched clothes.

'To think that my son is married to the sultan's daughter,' he used to say to himself, 'when I was once penniless.'

Regularly he used to fill a basket with the finest fruit and go out to the rock where he had first caught Abdullah from the Sea. Each time he shouted to him but he never came, and Abdullah had to carry the fruit back to his house again.

But this time he went further out to sea, to see if the man-fish would hear him from this lonely spot. He climbed out onto a rocky ledge and called,

'Abdullah from the Sea,
Abdullah there below,
Abdullah hear you me?
Abdullah from the Sea?
Abdullah from the Land
Upon the rock does stand,
With fruit to give to thee,
Abdullah from the Sea.'

Suddenly to Abdullah's joy, the sea became rough and the waves turned into a whirlpool, and from their midst rose Abdullah from the Sea.

'My old friend,' rejoiced Abdullah and gave the man-fish the fruit.

'The king of the sea will be glad,' said Abdullah from the Sea. 'He shared the

His gift was received with joy by Abdullah from the Sea.

fruit you gave me before. Fruit to us is like pearls to you. Wait there.'

And the man-fish dived with the basket of fruit below the waves. Soon he returned with the basket heaped up with coral and pearls.

'I owe so much of my good fortune to you,' said Abdullah from the Land, 'how can I ever repay you? I used to be a poor fisherman and now I am grand vizier. I wish I could bring you to the sultan's palace so you could meet him.'

'I should soon die out of the water,' said the man-fish.

'And I should die under the sea,' said Abdullah, 'though I should be most interested to meet the king of the sea.'

'That's easily arranged,' said the man-fish, and he dived below the waves.

Soon he reappeared above the water, holding a golden jar above his head.

'Take this,' he said, handing it to Abdullah from the Land.

'What is it?' asked Abdullah.

'If you smear this ointment all over your body you can follow me to the bottom of the sea.'

'But won't there be fierce sharks and octopuses which will attack me?' asked Abdullah from the Land timidly.

'They won't come near you while you are smeared with this, or if you are with me. So don't fear any danger.'

'Then I shall be honoured to come,' said Abdullah from the Land, and he began to take off his rich clothes and turban. He only kept on a loin cloth. Then he smeared the mysterious ointment from the jar over his face and arms and chest.

Abdullah from the Sea helped cover his back, with cold fishy hands. The ointment seemed to give off a vapour that Abdullah from the Land inhaled as he glided swiftly after Abdullah from the Sea, deep into the water.

It was strange and dark at first, but then he began to look about him. He was in a green watery world and he could see shoals of fish flitting by.

'How much further is it?' he asked, swimming fast and easily after the flashing figure of the man-fish as he glided down and down.

Soon he reappeared above the water, holding a golden jar above his head.

They were in a great vault with caves in its sides.

'Here we are!' said Abdullah from the Sea. They were in a great vault with caves in its sides. Abdullah from the Land gazed with wonder at the glorious sea shells and strange and splendid fish with silver and rainbow-coloured scales swimming all around them.

He could see shimmering sea stars and sea horses and strange blooms and plants that softly waved to and fro in the sea. And from all sides came men from the sea swimming to look at this extraordinary creature their friend had brought.

'A being without a tail, ha, ha, ha!'
laughed the king.

When the king of the sea saw Abdullah
from the Land, he began to laugh.

'Ha, ha!' he chuckled violently. 'Ho,
ho! What is this strange creature I see
with projections underneath instead of a
fish tail?'

'Those are his legs, sire,' said Abdullah from the Sea. 'He has them so he
can run upon the land.'

'Does he, ho, ho!' laughed the king.
'A being without a tail, ha, ha, ha! I have
never seen anything so funny before in my
life under the sea. Ha, ha, ha!'

The king of the sea made Abdullah from the Land turn round so that he could take another look at his legs, and each time he regarded them he shook again with laughter. All the other men from the sea laughed too, and Abdullah began to feel more and more foolish.

'Thank you for bringing this amazing creature to me, Abdullah from the Sea,' said the king, and he presented the man from the land with a handful of costly pearls as a souvenir of his visit.

Then he began laughing again.

Above the water the two Abdullahs parted from each other.

'I'm afraid that you were insulted, my good friend,' said Abdullah from the Sea, 'and had an embarrassing time.'

'O my friend, if I took you to my sultan, and people, they would be sure to be equally silly about your tail.'

'I suppose we must each stay where we belong, you on the land and I deep under the sea. So we must part.'

'Farewell, Abdullah from the Sea.'
'Farewell, Abdullah from the Land.'

'Farewell, Abdullah from the Land.'

The Little Golden Fish

Long ago in a distant country lived an old fisherman with his wife. They were very poor, and their house near the sea was made out of a jar.

It looked strange but they had made it comfortable with everything they needed. The roof across the opening at the top of the jar was covered with stones, to weigh it down in sea gales.

There was a long porch which kept the house shady and cool from the sun, and a seat outside where, when their work was done, the fisherman and his wife could have a rest, talking of this and that.

The house was on top of the cliffs and in front of it was a gap with the sea surging far below. But in his youth the fisherman had built a fine bridge across the gap out of tree trunks sawn in half nailed on to beams.

He crossed this bridge to go out fishing every day, his wife hung out her washing along it too.

This bridge saved them both a lot of trouble. He would have had to go a long way round to get to the sea, and his wife would have had to climb up and down the cliffs to hang out the socks.

You can tell they had been living in this house for a very long time, all their married life in fact.

In all those years the little old fisherman caught fish for a living. Some they used to bake for supper, and eat with bread baked by the fisherman's wife, and if there was any left over the old man used to sell it in the market.

It used to give them just enough money to live on. The fisherman's wife was rather grumpy about being so poor, but he was used to her nature, and on the whole they enjoyed their lives by the sea and in their quaint house.

Then one day things began to go wrong for the fisherman. He began not to catch any fish in his nets and jars.

At first he couldn't believe it. He thought it must be because of the cold weather if the skies were grey . . . and because of the hot weather if the skies were blue.

He tried different kinds of bait, worms and flies and sugared crusts, but every day his nets were empty when he hauled them in from the sea.

'I don't understand it,' he said to his wife, for she began to complain when he came back night after night with no fish to eat or sell.

Soon the beans and flour in the store-cupboard were eaten, and the day came when there was not a crumb in the larder,

and no money to buy anything.

'Don't come back until you've caught something,' his wife shouted after him crossly as he set off across the bridge with

'Don't come back until you've caught something,' shouted the fisherman's wife.

his jars and nets on his back.

'I won't,' he said as he walked away. 'I certainly won't. I am going to stay by the sea and cast my nets night and day until I do catch something.'

'I should think so too,' his wife shouted after him. 'There are fish in the market on sale. So there must be some fish in the sea.'

Suddenly he felt a huge pull on his net.

Three times that day the fisherman hauled his nets in as light as air. He refused to give in. 'I'm staying here from dawn to dusk, by sun or moon until I catch a fish,' he shouted.

Suddenly he felt a huge pull on his net. He must have caught a shoal of mackerel! But when using all his strength he dragged in the net, it was empty, except for a glint of gold.

In the net a little golden fish lay flipping its tail, and gasping.

The fisherman bent down and took it in his hand, where it implored him with its eyes. It was incredibly heavy.

'You're a fine little fish,' said the fisherman, 'your scales look as though they are made of gold like the king's crown. I don't know what you have inside you, but I can hardly carry you.'

Then to his astonishment the fish spoke to him with a human voice.

'Kind fisherman, throw me back in the sea and I will grant you anything you wish.'

'Kind fisherman, throw me back into the sea and I will grant you anything you wish.'

The fisherman was stiff with fright, but then he said, 'Of course. I think you're too good to eat. Here you go!'

That evening his wife greeted him with, 'Where's the fish for supper?'

The fisherman clapped his hand over his mouth. He had forgotten it entirely in his thoughts about the golden fish.

'I only caught one fish,' he said, 'a magic fish made of gold which spoke to me with a human voice.'

'The man's losing his senses,' said his wife. 'Magic? How magic?'

'It said if I threw it back into the sea it would grant me any wish.'

'So what did you wish for?' asked his wife. 'A catch of herring? Money?'

'Then go straight back and ask it for something,' said his wife.

'And what does your wife wish for?'

'Why, nothing,' said the fisherman.

'Then go straight back and ask it for something,' said his wife.

'Ask it for what?' asked the old man.

'Ask it . . ask it . . for a new wash-tub for me,' said his wife thinking fast. 'You spared his life, that's worth a new wash-tub.'

The fisherman went back to the sea shore very, very unwillingly. He felt sure the golden fish would not like to be asked for a new wash-tub. He went close up to the waves and called:

'Golden fish in the sea,
Can you hear me in the deep?
Grant my wife one wish for me,
And I will forever happy keep.'
The golden fish appeared.

'And what does your wife wish for?'

'A new wash-tub, please, golden one.'

'Go back to your house. Your wish is granted.'

And the golden fish swam away deep into the water in the flash of an eye.

'I've never seen a more splendid wash-tub,' gasped the fisherman.

The old fisherman climbed up the steps from the shore and ran across the bridge and into his house.

There in the middle of the room was an enormous tub complete with a tap.

'I've never seen such a splendid wash-tub,' gasped the fisherman. 'Is it not good of the golden fish?'

'I suppose so,' said his wife. 'A new wash-tub is always useful. But if I had had time to think, I should have asked for something much bigger.'

'But my beloved wife,' said the old man, 'I can't ask for anything else. Why not be glad that you've got this new wash-tub. Isn't that lucky enough?'

'What I should wish for is a better house,' she said, 'I'm tired of living in a jar. For years and years I've wanted to change.'

Argue with her as he tried, she would not give in, and very slowly the fisherman went back to the water's edge. He hesitated for a long time, then called out:

'Golden fish in the sea,
Can you hear me in the deep?
Grant my wife one wish for me,
And I will forever happy keep.'

The golden fish appeared, its head above the water.

'Well, fisherman, what does your wife wish for now?'

The fisherman said apologetically, 'My wife would like to have a better house, if it please you, golden fish.'

'Go home. Her wish is granted.' And the fish disappeared in the waves.

The fisherman went back up the rocks from the sea-shore and towards the place where he and his wife had lived all their married lives.

When he came up over a high point from which he could see his house, he nearly fell off the top of the rock he was standing on.

Where the house made out of a jar had been now stood a pretty new house, with green shutters and a green door.

The golden fish appeared, its head above the water.

'I can't believe it,' he cried, and ran down to look closer. He hardly dared open the door, but at last he took courage and went inside.

It was all shining, brand new, with check curtains and rugs on the floor and a pine table and chairs.

'How could a house like this appear in one moment?' the fisherman murmured. 'One minute a jar, and the next all this!'

He found his wife wearing her best clothes sitting on the verandah at the back of the house and swinging on a new rocking chair. There was a fine view of the sea from here.

The fisherman looked all round him. 'Is there anything anyone could wish for more than this?'

His wife replied, 'Oh yes, I am quite pleased now. A house is better than a wash-tub. I'm glad I sent you back to ask for it.'

The fisherman felt contented with life as he promised the golden fish.

Before long, it is sad to say, the fisherman's wife began to find fault with her new house.

There stood a pretty new house, with green shutters and a green door.

In the end he gave in and went back to the sea-shore.

'It could be bigger,' she said, with a wave of her hand at the room. 'I like it. It is a comfortable little house if your taste is for poky places, but one can't entertain one's friends here, and I still have to do the housework myself.'

The little old fisherman became rather stubborn then.

'But my dear, I told the golden fish that if he granted your wish for a new house, that would content me for ever. You will have to be glad of this because I cannot ask him for anything else.'

'I don't see why not,' said his wife. 'I want a house with servants. I was never suited to being a fisherman's wife. I know this is a pleasant little house, but I want one more suitable for a dignified lady. I refuse to pass all my days in this humble way.'

The fisherman tried not to give way to his wife, but every day she nagged about her latest wish, and persisted that she was sure the golden fish would not refuse him.

'It has never refused you so far? How do you know it will refuse now? It might be quite happy to give me the house I require with servants and silk sheets if you ask. A little wish like that would be nothing to such a magical golden fish. Whatever you have asked for so far has appeared, bang; as if out of a puff of air. One minute I was in a house made out of a jar and looking at a new wash-tub. The next I was sitting in this place in my best dress.'

In the end he gave in and went back to the sea shore. He stood up and shouted:

'Golden fish in the sea,
Can you hear me in the deep?
Grant my wife one wish for me,
And I will forever happy keep.'

Instantly the golden fish appeared before him in the water.

'What does your wife wish for now, fisherman?'

'A grand house for a dignified lady with servants, if it please you, golden fish.'

'Her wish is granted for the last time.'

'Her wish is granted for the last time.'

The fisherman wondered what he would see when he went back this time. He ran back to his house, then stopped.

In place of the little house with the green shutters there stood a magnificent

At the top of a flight of marble stairs stood a
lady in rich clothes surrounded by servants.

mansion. At the top of a flight of marble steps stood a lady in rich clothes surrounded by servants.

'She can't be my wife,' thought the fisherman, as he ran up the stairs towards her.

When she came closer he realized she was his wife! He began to wave his hand around at the mansion and the grounds, when one of the servants stepped out.

'Anyone who wishes to speak to the lady of the house, has to ask for an appointment,' he said to the old man.

'But she's my wife!' he said. Yet no one listened, so he went and sat down on the steps.

Soon a servant came to him and said,

'Your supper will be served to you in the kitchen and a bed has been made up for you in the gardener's shed. My lady will see you in the morning.'

The food was rich, but the little fisherman could not eat. Nor sleep.

In the morning he was led before his wife by a servant. He hardly knew her in her grand clothes and wig.

'This is quite a good mansion,' said his wife, 'but I have decided I want to be a queen. You must go and ask your magic fish to make me into a queen and provide me with a castle.'

'The fish said that your wish for this mansion was the last he would grant to me,' said her husband. 'I dare not.'

'Do as I say or I'll have you thrown out,' said his wife, 'never to come back.'

The little fisherman returned to the sea and sighed many times on the way. He went close to the waves and called:

'*You must go and ask your magic fish to make me into a queen,*' *demanded his wife.*

'Golden fish in the sea,
Can you hear me in the deep?
Grant my wife one wish for me,
And I will forever happy keep.'
The fish instantly appeared.
'What does your wife wish for now, fisherman?'
The fisherman hardly dared to tell the fish. He twisted his hat round and round in his hands.
'She wishes to be a queen with a great castle if it please you, golden fish.'

He hid in some bushes and saw his wife dressed as a queen.

The golden fish became angry.

'This is the last wish I shall grant you for your wife, fisherman. Go back to your home. Her wish is granted.'

And the fish turned and swam below the waves with a glitter of gold and vanished.

The fisherman went back from the sea and when he got nearer to where the mansion had been, he could see the high stately towers of a great castle.

He went up to the wall surrounding it and hid in some bushes. There he saw his wife dressed as a queen surrounded by courtiers.

When he went towards her across the lawn, a sentry stepped out and pointed his halberd at him.

'Let him approach,' said the old man's wife to one of her courtiers. He told the page and the page told the sentry and so the fisherman was allowed to come close up to her. He bowed deeply and his wife smiled at him most graciously.

'I am pleased with the arrangements your fish has made for me,' she said. And she nodded for him to leave.

The old fisherman had his food in the kitchen and slept in the shed in a bed which had been made up for him among the potted geraniums.

He only saw his wife from time to time when she walked round in great dignity, surrounded by all the people of the court bowing and curtseying.

'At least she is contented now,' said the little fisherman. 'There is nothing more she can wish for.'

Then one day he was summoned from the kitchen where he was eating his supper. He followed the footman through the many carpeted corridors and passed

The wind began to howl and the trees bent double under its force.

through gilded rooms where people were waiting to see the queen.

At last he was ushered in before her. She was sitting on a high throne and looked down at him.

'I am quite pleased with being queen and with this fine castle, but I have discovered that I can become an even greater being. I want to be ruler of the sun, the stars and the moon. I wish to reign over heaven and earth.'

The little fisherman shook his head. 'I cannot ask such a thing. The fish said that

I have had my last wish for you.'

'If you don't do what I say,' cried his wife in a shrill, commanding voice, 'I shall send for my guards and have you locked up. I am queen and everyone obeys me, and so must you.'

The fisherman bowed and was led from her presence by soldiers and taken to the castle gates.

He began to walk towards the sea. As he went, the black clouds in the sky piled up and there were flashes of lightning. The wind began to howl and the trees bent double under its force.

The little fisherman became scared. He began to run and soon came to the sea. The sky was black and menacing as he knelt on the sea shore and called out:

'Golden fish in the sea,
Can you hear me in the deep?
Grant my wife one wish for me,
And I will forever happy keep.'

The golden fish rose from the waves and looked at him.

'What does your wife wish for now, fisherman?'

The fisherman hesitated then said:

'She wishes to rule over the sun and moon and stars; over heaven and earth, if it please you, golden fish.'

The golden fish spoke in a solemn fearful voice:

'Go back to your house, fisherman. Your wife is given what she deserves.'

And the fish disappeared in a streak of gold. The fisherman went back home slowly, wondering what he would find now.

'Go back to your house, fisherman. Your wife is given what she deserves.'

As he climbed up from the shore he saw that the broad avenues belonging to the castle had gone.

There was the old bridge made of trees sawn in half, and there . . . there was the old house back again, the house made out of a jar. His wife was standing in the doorway as she used to.

The fisherman went up to the house expecting to be met with a loud grumble but she came and kissed him and said:

'We have our old house back, husband, and I'm so pleased.'

The fisherman went back home slowly . . .

But there was a great change in her. Now she never grumbled.

Not one thing the fish had granted in answer to her wishes had been left. Even the new wash-tub had vanished.

The fisherman was pleased when he saw that his wife was back to the old ways again, busy and bustling. But there was a great change in her. Now she never grumbled.

Every day he took his nets and his jars and went down to the seashore to catch fish. He cast his nets out and usually when he drew them in there were plaice and flounder and sole lying at the bottom.

He sold the spare fish in the market, and she baked the bread, and they lived happily together in the old house.

Often the little old fisherman stood looking deep into the water to see if he could catch sight of the golden fish. But he never saw him again.

The Three Little Pigs

There were once three pigs called Oliver, Gilbert and William. They were fine, hungry young pigs who always ate every scrap of food from their plates, and liked nothing better than the peel as well as the potatoes.

Consequently every day they grew fatter and larger, and living with them in the family sty became something of a squash for their sixteen little brothers and sisters.

Mrs Pig, their mother, did her best to see that every one in her large crowd of piglets had a share of dinner and room to play games, but even for her it became too much.

The day came when she called Oliver, Gilbert and William to her and said, 'I'm sorry my sons, but I'm afraid that you will all three have to go out into the world and seek your fortunes. I can no longer keep you. Every day you need more to eat, and besides you can see for yourselves that the sty we live in is not large enough to hold us all any more.'

Oliver, Gilbert and William well understood her problem and though they were sad to leave her, and all their little brothers and sisters, and the farm where they were born, they were excited at the thought of going into the wide world.

At first they had some adventurous ideas such as going to Australia or joining the merchant navy . . . ideas which made Mrs Pig extremely nervous and say that if she had known they were going to be so wild she would never have suggested their going in the first place.

'What I had in mind, my sons, was that you should each build yourself a house, somewhere not too far away from here, where I can hear news of you and perhaps come and visit you.'

Oliver, Gilbert and William were rather disappointed about giving up going to Australia, but then they all grew very excited about building their own houses.

The local builder lent them a book of house plans, and soon they were busy planning the most amazing homes, with tiled bathrooms and sun terraces.

They trotted over to the yard with the builder who picked out various tools and handy items like nails for them. But best of all he gave them a ladder of their own.

Before they left, their mother called them to her and said:

'I want you to promise that when you build your houses you will make them strong enough to keep the bad wolf out. He is always watching for pigs like you to eat for supper!'

'We promise, mother!' they said, and saying good-bye they went on their way.

They each had a delightful new hat for a parting present. Oliver's had a wide brim with a long feather. He was rather a dressy pig.

Gilbert had a tweed fishing hat, which he felt was suitable for wearing in all weathers when travelling. And William had a cap with a large peak, to keep the sun out of his eyes when he was building his house.

They carried the ladder the builder had given them between them and shared out the building tools. Oliver carried a satchel with food in it for the journey, provided by their mother.

The three little pigs walked along the road singing and talking, all the time looking for a suitable place to build their houses. They walked round this way and that and at last came to a place they all liked.

It was grassy, with the farm fields nearby and an orchard not far away. By now they were beginning to get tired and hungry, so this perhaps helped make up their minds for them.

'Before we decide how we're going to begin, and which plot we can each have,' said Gilbert, who was always enormously hungry, 'let's eat.'

'A good idea,' said Oliver and William. So they opened up the satchel and looked inside for the crusty rolls and cheese and potatoes their mother had packed.

After they had eaten they talked over the types of houses they were going to build.

Oliver said, lying back on the grass, 'I don't think I'll bother with a floor, the grass is so soft here. And I won't have a ceiling either. The sky is so blue, it would be nice to look at it.'

'You remember what you promised our mother,' said William severely. 'You

must build a strong house to keep out the bad wolf. So it must have a roof.'

After they had each settled on their plot, they got to work busily. Oliver decided to build his house from bamboo. He found a clump of bamboo canes and cut off a stack of long pieces with a little hacksaw from his tool kit.

He decided that he wanted to move in that night and set about tying the canes together to make walls like screens. He used string and scissors and glue and was very proud of his elegant residence.

But he found the work tiring. So he paused to have another picnic. However, his house was ready in good time for supper and to sleep in.

A little way away, Gilbert had begun to collect materials for a house made from pine wood.

The three little pigs walked along the road looking for a suitable place to build their houses.

Oliver decided to built his house from bamboo.

Gilbert sank back on to a tree stump and drank some lemonade through a straw.

Unfortunately to get the wood he had to cut down a large tree! Then he had to saw it lengthwise into planks. He almost regretted choosing wood. Phew! He had thought it would be easy to make a wooden house. What a lot of work!

When he was through with stacking up the planks, Gilbert wiped his forehead and sank back on to the tree stump and drank some lemonade through a straw.

'I wish I'd known what to expect went into making a house out of wood planks! I'd have settled on a log cabin if I had known. Then I could just have cut up branches!'

He had to rest for hours to get enough strength back to carry on, but once he got going again, he began to take a pride in making his house look nice.

He finished after supper ready to move in and was proud of the neat chalet he had built, with a window and a door and a deep gutter from the pitched roof. He even painted a flower on the front of the gable.

The trouble was that although Gilbert's chalet was delightful at a distance, it was rather shaky close to, and somewhat short on nails through the planks, and the frame was inclined to lean in different directions.

'Do you think it's strong enough?' asked William. 'It's lovely—but isn't it

just a little wobbly?'

'Of course it will wobble it you shake it,' said Gilbert. 'It's a wooden house, not a brick and stone one like yours.'

William was using some bricks the builder had said he could have. His house was strong with a tiled roof.

That night, each of the three pigs was able to sleep in his own house, though

William was using some bricks the builder said he could have.

William's was still unfinished. He still had to build the chimney and plaster the outside walls.

Oliver and Gilbert thought he was being fussy. They sat in their own houses admiring them and thinking how dull William's was by comparison with their own wooden buildings.

The following morning Oliver was leaning against his stove having a rest when he saw a great hairy hand on his door and heard a gruff voice saying:

'Piglet, my friend, let me come in.'

Oliver replied nervously:

'Never. I know who you are, wolf. I

Oliver saw a great hairy hand on his door and heard a gruff voice . . .

was warned about you by my mother, and I promised never to open the door to you, because you eat pigs up!'

'If you don't let me come in little piglet,' said the harsh voice, 'then by the hair of my chinny-chin-chin, I'll *huff* and I'll *puff* and I'll *blow* your house down. And then I'll come in and gobble you up!'

With that, Oliver heard the sound of a mighty wind like a hurricane. His walls, his stove, his hat and even he himself were all blown away by the huge puff the wolf blew.

Oliver had to run for his life with the wolf's breath behind him.

His walls and his stove and his hat and even he himself were all blown away.

He had just time to grab his hat and race for his brothers as hard as his trotters would go. Gilbert's wooden chalet was nearest.

'Gilbert! Gilbert!' yelled Oliver. 'Quick, open the door. The wolf is just behind me!'

The wolf's hairy hand just missed him, as Gilbert undid the latch, opened the door and hauled Oliver inside. The door closed right in the wolf's face which was so near that he ran into it.

'Quick, bolt the door,' panted Oliver, 'and push some furniture against it. He's a very large wolf.'

'Never mind,' said Gilbert, 'you'll be safe in here.'

'Are you sure?' asked Oliver, watching the walls rattle and shake, as the wolf went all round the outside pushing them, and growling.

'Oh, never fear,' smiled Gilbert, 'this is a wooden house, and wood is much stronger than bamboo cane, and nails are stronger than glue and string.'

At this moment the wolf stopped outside the front door and nuzzled it. Oliver and Gilbert clung to each other, trembling from head to trotters and curly tails.

'Little pigs, little pigs, let me come in,' growled the wolf fiercely.

'Never!!' quavered Gilbert as bravely as he could, watching the door shake.

'If you don't let me come in little piglets,' growled the wolf horribly, 'then by the hair of my chinny-chin-chin, I'll *huff* and I'll *puff* and I'll *blow* your house down. And then I'll come in and gobble you up!'

'Oh! Ow!' cried Oliver and Gilbert.

They heard the wolf drawing a deep breath and saw from the window his chest swell up as big as a balloon and then they heard the sound of a great rushing wind.

The zinc piping chimney flew off and the roof with them hanging from the rafter. The wolf was only a few yards away from them, but luckily for them he was so winded by the huge blow it took him a minute or two to chase them.

'Help! Help!' they both squealed. 'Help! William, unlock your door, the wolf is after us!'

The roof flew off with them hanging from the rafter.

'Quick, open the door !' yelled Oliver. 'The
wolf is just behind me !'

They tore across the garden with the wolf on his way now to catch them. With his long bounding steps, the two pigs were going to be in trouble if William had gone out leaving his door locked.

But William had seen what was happening from his upstairs window.

'The front door is open,' he called down. 'Come right in and bolt the door!'

'The front door is open,' William called down.

126

Oliver and Gilbert were just in time to slam the door and lock it as the wolf came rushing round the corner. They heard him outside snuffling after them.

William came down the stairs and took his brothers into the living room. Then he

went round putting the shutters across the windows and making sure all the bolts and catches were secure.

He could see the wolf prowling round angrily, trying to find a way in to the sturdy little house with its heavy tiled roof.

'But what if he is strong enough to blow your house down,' groaned Oliver peeping out of the keyhole at the wolf.

'Don't worry,' said William. 'This house is a fortress. 'Why, I've even put bars across the windows!'

'Oh, William you are sensible.' said his brothers. 'If only we had kept our promise to our dear mother and built our houses strongly like this!'

'I had no idea he was so large and powerful,' said Gilbert, whimpering and stealing a look at the wolf after Oliver through the keyhole. 'With his teeth he could eat the three of us in three gulps.'

'Look!' cried Oliver. 'He's taking a deep breath ready to blow. No, he isn't, he's coming over to the door! You can feel his hot breath through the crack!'

Then the wolf shouted from where he was standing:

The wolf stood well back and puffed up his chest and began to blow.

'Little pigs, little pigs, let me come in.'

'Never!' shouted William through the keyhole.

The wolf laughed.

'Then you know what to expect. I blew down your brother's bamboo cane house, and I blew down your brother's wooden house, and now I shall blow down your house.'

'Do your best, bad wolf!' shouted William, while his brothers began to cry and clasp each other with terror.

'Little pigs, little pigs, let me come in,' shouted the wolf again, 'or by the hair of my chinny-chin-chin, I'll *huff* and I'll *puff* and I'll *blow* your house down, and then I shall come in and gobble you up!'

Now the wolf stood well back, and puffed up his chest as he drew in a deep breath and then he began to blow.

The whistling and rushing sound of his breath whirled round the chimney like a typhoon. It was as though a storm had blown up. Outside the birds were nearly blown away, the shovels flew up in the air and the lantern was hurled off its bracket.

But the house did not move an inch. The wolf's efforts were all in vain.

The three little pigs saw the wolf stop blowing and look back at the house with his fist clenched.

'What's the matter? Beaten, wolf?' cried William through the front door. 'You didn't think you could blow down this house did you? You won't be able to push it over either. This house is as strong as a castle!'

And he and his brothers laughed and hugged each other and danced about.

'Look, the wolf is slinking away. But if I know him, he's only gone away to try to think of another way of catching us. A wolf like him is extra cunning when it comes to getting at young pork!'

William was right. The next day the wolf came back. The three pigs heard him go round to the rear of the house, and then his knock on the back door.

'Did you hear?' whispered Oliver. 'He knocked. He thinks we'll open it for him!'

The wolf knocked again and called,

The wolf was determined to have the three little pigs for breakfast, dinner and tea.

'I've come to visit you my friends. I know you are too clever for me so I've given up any idea of catching you.'

The pigs inside pulled a face at each other when they heard this and chuckled so he could not hear.

Trying not to giggle they said:

'We still won't open the door, wolf.'

'I'm so lonely,' he went on, 'and I was hoping that you would be three new friends for me to play with.'

He spoke in honeyed tones.

This idea was so funny that it was a long time before the three pigs could answer him, for they were laughing so much.

'If you want friends,' they called back, 'you should try to stop gobbling people up and huffing and puffing at their houses.'

But the wolf was determined to have the three little pigs for breakfast, dinner and tea, so he tried again.

'I noticed yesterday that you had a basket of apples in your garden, so I presume you like apples?'

'Yes,' chorused the three pigs.

'I suppose you've noticed the orchard across the meadow?'

'Yes. We shall go there when you go away,' said William.

'But there's one big apple tree in the orchard where the apples taste better, and are juicier than on any of the other trees in the orchard. Why don't you let me help you pick some apples from that tree for you, with my long reach.'

'He's thinking of pork with apple sauce,' whispered William. 'Let's pretend to go and trick him instead.'

Oliver and Gilbert weren't too sure, but they heard William say:

'Very well, it seems a good idea.

The wolf looked up in the tree and saw the three little pigs in its branches.

Where shall we meet and at what time?'

Through the window they could see the wolf smile and lick his lips and bare his sharp long white teeth:

'Come to the orchard at noon, to the tall apple tree in the farthest corner, and I'll meet you there.'

'All right then, noon it is. But, we'll be there earlier,' whispered William.

The next morning the three little pigs crept out of William's house two hours

earlier than they had said they would to meet the wolf. Soon they were up in the tree picking apples.

Unfortunately, the wolf had had the same idea. He came along one hour before noon when they were still up the tree.

'The wolf!' they whispered. 'Now what shall we do?'

The wolf looked up in the tree and saw the three little pigs in its branches.

'Oh wolf, good morning; we're just coming down. But here's an apple for you,' and William threw an apple as far as he could.

'Catch!' he shouted. 'It is the most beautiful apple on the tree.

'Here's an apple for you,' shouted William. 'Catch!'

They ran to William's house as fast as their fat little legs would carry

The wolf was taken in and ran after the apple.

'Quick!' said William to the others. 'Down the tree quietly and slip off home as fast as you can go.'

And one after another the three little pigs slithered down the tree and on to the ground. Then they ran to William's house as fast as their legs would carry them.

The wolf was picking up the apple and

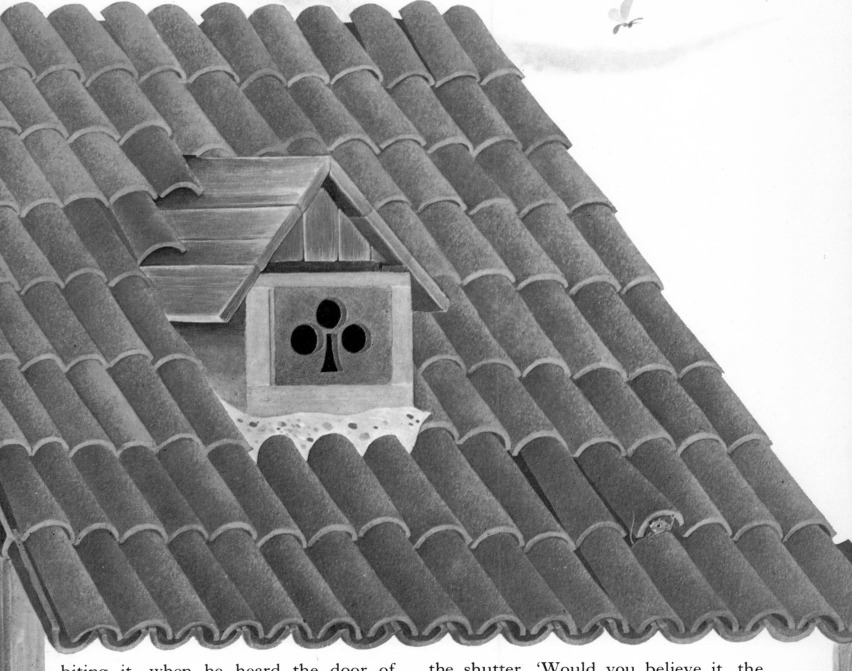

'He's still lurking around,' said William through the shutter.

biting it, when he heard the door of William's house bang shut on the pigs.

'That was a near thing,' Oliver said as he leaned up against the door, out of breath.

'Too close for me,' gasped Gilbert.

'He's still lurking around,' said William looking out through a chink in the shutter. 'Would you believe it, the impudence of that wolf!'

'What's he doing?' asked the others.

'Only taking our ladder and putting it up against our roof!'

'Oooh!' cried Oliver and Gilbert, 'it's no good, he won't give in until he's got to us and when he does he'll eat us up with

135

They saw a huge hairy foot pass the window on the ladder.

those great teeth!'

'We shall have to stop him then.'

'He's climbing on the roof,' said William, 'that determined old bad wolf. We shall have to teach him a lesson he won't forget, so that he will leave us alone in future.'

'But how, William?'

'You'll see. Come on, we must light a fire in the hearth and make it blaze up as quickly and fiercely as we can.'

'The smoke might drive him away, you mean?' asked Oliver.

'I think it might take more than smoke,' answered William. 'Oliver, if you bring the sticks and Gilbert lays them I can keep a watch on the wolf.'

William kept a lookout from the window and watched the other two pigs light the fire, and blow up the flames by pumping air at them from the bellows.

The fire was burning brightly and sending tongues of fire up the chimney when they saw a huge hairy foot pass the window on the ladder.

'He's going to try to get to us by the roof,' said William, 'but he won't be able to break through those tiles. I chose the heaviest the builder had to spare in his yard. Believe me, it was hard work carrying those tiles up the ladder—but I'm glad I did now!'

'Then how can the wolf think of getting inside the house from the roof?' asked Gilbert.

William smiled and pointed at the fire.

'I think we'll fill the kettle to hang on the hook over the fire to make us all some tea, but we won't start to boil it yet.'

The three little pigs waited for the next move of the wolf. If they didn't stop him this time . . !

His long shaggy tail hung dangerously over the flames of the fire.

The three little pigs took their places. Gilbert climbed into the dustbin with the lid lifted on one side so he could see out.

Oliver crouched behind the fire guard, and William stretched out along the mantelshelf.

They heard a slithering sound on the roof and a cry as the wolf almost slipped. Then they heard him puffing and breathing hard as he squashed himself into the chimney.

'Supposing he gets stuck!' whispered Oliver, and they all chuckled.

Then they heard a loud coughing and sneezing and scrabbling. Then suddenly they heard a great sliding noise and the wolf's harsh voice crying out 'Owwww! Owwww! Help, help, help!'

His great hairy foot and red trousers came out of the chimney with a rush, and his long shaggy tail hung dangerously over the flames of the fire.

'OOOOOWWWWWWWWWWW!' he yelled, and came running and tumbling into the room and out of the front door.

They ran to the door, and saw the wolf

'Ooowwwwwww!' yelled the big bad wolf.

rush over to the pond and sit with his tail dangling in the water.

'I think he'll leave us alone from now on,' said William, 'though we shall have to keep an eye on him always.'

'Wolves will always fancy pigs,' remarked Gilbert, 'it's their nature.'

'He's probably a bit of a coward,' said William, 'and won't think we're quite so easy to catch from this day.'

He hung the kettle over the fire.

'Now, you two must live with me until you've rebuilt your houses.'

'And we'll make ours as strong as yours this time, William. You'll see. We've learned our lesson!'

'I think he'll leave us alone from now on,' said William.

The Seven Ravens

In a land far away, and long ago, lived a father and mother who had seven sons. In that country the number seven was considered lucky, and the couple were thought fortunate to have seven fine children.

In spite of this, they hoped they would have a daughter. It was their dream. And the people in the village wished the same but for different reasons.

The seven sons were so naughty, always up trees and falling in the river or scuffling and fighting, that the villagers thought it would be a good thing for everyone if a little girl came into the family.

'It might help to make things in this village a little quieter,' they said to each other as they watched the seven brothers tumbling and chasing each other past their peaceful houses.

But winter followed summer and the years went by, and still the couple saw no sign of another child. Then one day, the wife realized that she was going to have another baby in the spring.

'Of course it's sure to be another boy,' the parents told everybody. 'We've always had sons before you see, so we expect the new baby will be another son.'

But . . . wonder of wonders . . . when spring came the baby was a girl.

The parents and the people of the village were so delighted that they had a feast that lasted for three days.

But alas, although the brothers were healthy and strong, the baby girl, their new little sister, was delicate.

The parents did not want to think that perhaps she was frail because she was their eighth child and had taken away the luck from their house.

The doctor came to see her and upset the father and mother deeply when he told them solemnly that he did not think that the child would have long to live.

He advised them that the baby should be christened at once, as in those days a baby might not be saved so easily as nowadays.

The father called his seven sons to him and gave the eldest an earthenware pitcher.

'We shall need some water for the christening,' he said. 'Fill this at the well and make haste to bring it back here without spilling any. I meanwhile will go and ask the priest to perform the ceremony.'

The seven brothers left their father and gathered outside the door of their house arguing quietly because of the baby being so weak.

'I don't see why you should be the only one to carry the christening water for the baby,' said the second eldest.

'Nor do I,' said the next brother. 'I don't see why we all shouldn't share in it. It's important to us too.'

'I think we should all carry water for the sister who belongs to us all equally,' said another.

In the end they each took an earthenware pitcher from the kitchen and went with the oldest brother to the well.

When their father came out, the others hid the pitchers under their coats. Only the eldest son kept his in his hand. He didn't give his brothers away, though he was annoyed with them for trying to take his privileges.

'Don't delay,' called the father. 'It is urgent that you bring the water back as quickly as you can.'

The brothers hurried along trying to race each other to the well, and by pushing each other out of the way and scrambling to get ahead by the time they reached it two of them had dropped their pitchers and broken them.

'I am the first to draw the water,' said the oldest brother, pushing his brothers aside. 'Our father sent me to bring the water back and you just came along.'

'Not so,' said his brothers angrily. 'We have just as much right as you to bring water for the baby's christening,' and they all began to fight each other.

The result of this was that two more pitchers were broken and another pitcher fell down the well.

This left the eldest brother and the youngest with a pitcher each.

'I say I go first,' said the oldest brother fastening his pitcher to the rope.

'No. I am the smallest. I should be the one,' cried the youngest brother, trying to fasten his pitcher to the well rope at the same time.

Both of the pitchers were knocked out of their hands and fell down into the well, where they echoed a sound of the splash as they hit the wall deep down.

The brothers looked at each other.

'Now what are we going to do?' they wondered.

'Father will beat us for sure,' said the second eldest. 'He is so anxious about the baby. And the priest is waiting.

The seven sons stood silently together.

'I don't dare go home without the water,' said one.

'Nor do I,' said another.

'Then how do you think I feel?' said the oldest brother, 'when he sent me.'

And they sat on the grass by the well wondering what to do.

At home their father and mother were waiting for them to come back. The priest had come and the doctor was still present. Though the father looked often along the road to see if his seven sons were returning with the water he could see no sign of them.

He would have set out to find them, but he could not leave his wife and baby.

'Those scoundrels, playing at a time like this!' he shouted in a temper. 'I wish that they could be changed into ravens!'

He did not mean it, but his wish worked. By the well his seven sons had disappeared, and in their place seven large ravens were hopping around, cawing at each other.

The strange thing was that from the day her brothers disappeared the baby girl began to recover. She grew into a healthy

He did not mean it but his wish worked, and his seven sons were turned into ravens.

She grew into a healthy little girl, with two pigtails and her own pet cat.

little girl, with two pigtails and her own pet cat.

Her parents loved her very much and spoilt her with presents of dolls and new dresses. But they did not tell her that once she had had seven brothers who had mysteriously vanished on the day she was christened.

The father had never mentioned that he had wished his sons to be turned into ravens. So when in spring seven of these birds, huge and black with yellow beaks came to settle in the branches of an apple tree outside the house, he wondered for a moment whether they could have anything to do with his wish. But he dismissed the thought. He felt guilt inside all the same.

The little girl loved the ravens who sat in the branches of the apple tree. Her bedroom window was across from the tree and

She kissed her parents good-bye and set out.

she used to talk to them and give them crusts of bread.

'Why do you think they like coming to our tree?' she once asked her father, and he replied, 'Because we feed them.'

One day the ravens flew away and the next spring did not return. The little girl missed them sadly. As she was alone in her family with no brothers or sisters to play with, she had treated the seven ravens like her dearest friends.

Then one day she heard some people from the village talking about her seven brothers.

'My brothers. I do not have any brothers!' thought the little girl.

She hurried home to her father and mother, very excited.

'I heard them saying in the village that I used to have seven brothers. Where are they?'

Her parents wished she had not found out the secret, but then they told her about the day of the christening.

'I never understood how they could have vanished so completely,' said her mother sadly.

Then the father for the first time confessed about his wish that the sons should be changed into ravens.

'My ravens!' cried the little girl. 'My brothers! I'm going to find them.'

The only things she took with her for her journey were a ring from her mother, a loaf of bread and some water.

She kissed her parents good-bye, and set out along the road.

As she walked along she thought to herself that if the ravens were her brothers, she wondered how she would be able to change them back into boys.

She travelled across wide plains where the land was flat. She went over hills and high up through the mountains in the heat of the sun and by the light of the moon and the stars.

Whenever she met anybody, she asked, 'Have you seen seven brothers who are probably seven ravens?'

But every one she spoke to shook his head. 'Seven ravens you say? Or was it seven brothers? We haven't seen either.'

The little girl travelled so far and in countries where she could not speak the language, that in the end she could not tell where she was.

Then in a far country she saw on top of a steep mountain a strange house with smoke coming out of its chimney.

'I believe I have come to the end of the world,' she said, 'which is where that house is standing. I must find my brothers there, because I have looked in all the other places in vain.'

She went along the path towards the house, and began to climb up the steep track that led up to it. It had a thatched roof and was plainly lived in.

But it was a friendly looking place.

She came up the flagstone path that wound up through the hillocky front garden and went bravely up to the front door. It was open, but she tapped on it rat-a-tat-tat. No one answered her. She

listened. Not a sound could she hear inside but the clock ticking.

Carefully she pushed the door open a little way and peeped through the gap. There was no one in the room so she went inside.

She saw on top of a steep mountain a strange house with smoke coming out of its chimney.

All round the room were little tables and chairs, even a baby chair. They were ready for supper.

By the fire, seven pans of chicken and potatoes were steaming, waiting for their owners.

'What a huge family must live here,' thought the little girl. She felt very hungry and tasted a ladleful of soup which was simmering in the pot hanging above the flaming logs. The soup was delicious.

The little girl wandered into a bedroom full of little beds and sat down in a large armchair. She began to feel so sleepy that first she slipped over one way, and then she slipped over the other, and then she fell fast asleep.

After her long journey it was lovely to be able to sleep in this warm house. Before she drifted off the little girl said to herself, 'I am sure I shall be seeing my brothers in this nice house.'

But when at last she woke up, it was not seven brothers she saw, but seven little girls just like herself, jumping about on seven little beds and shouting, 'She's woken up! She's woken up!'

'Who are you?' asked the little girl.

'We're the children from the end of the world.'

Then the little girl told them all about her journey and the seven ravens.

'Seven ravens!' exclaimed the girls. They all exclaimed at once!

All round the room were little tables and chairs.

By the fire, seven pans of chicken and potatoes were steaming, waiting for their owners.

She saw seven little girls like herself on seven little beds.

'Every morning when we are at work tidying our house, seven ravens come. They eat all the scraps left over from the day before. We save them all we can because they have healthy appetites, but we are very fond of them.'

The little girl's heart began to beat fast. She had come right across the world and she felt sure that these ravens were her long-lost brothers.

Suddenly outside they heard 'Caw, caw, caw.' and they could see the black wings of the birds spread out as they wheeled over the house.

'Quickly, hide under this tablecloth,' said the oldest girl and hid the ravens' little sister under it.

The room was filled with great flapping wings as the ravens flew in and alighted. They perched and began to eat the scraps of the previous day's supper which the children from the end of the world had put out in the bowls.

The children approached the ravens who had now finished every scrap and were pecking the crumbs out of their feathers, and began to make a fuss of them. Then one of the ravens noticed the little girl.

'Look! There's a new girl.'

The little girl went up close to him and gently stroked her hand over his glossy head.

'Have we met before?' he asked.

The ravens gathered round her and put their heads on one side to look at her with their bright bird eyes.

'I know you well,' said the little girl.

'We seem to have seen you somewhere,' said the ravens, 'but where?'

'Do you remember a house with an apple tree, which had branches close to an

The ravens perched and
began to eat the scraps of
the previous day's supper.

153

The ravens cawed and cawed and hopped about with laughter.

upstairs window?' the little girl asked them.

The ravens stared at her.

'I can remember it,' said the largest raven. 'Do you others remember, the large apple tree we lived in last summer?'

And the other ravens nodded and said, 'Caw, caw, it was a fine tree. We used to swing in its branches in the wind.'

The raven went close to the little girl and stared at her.

'So what does this mean? Do you have something to tell us?'

'I live in that house,' said the little girl. 'Although I have been away from it for many weeks on a journey. I have been looking for you.'

'Looking for us!' cried the ravens.

'You are my brothers,' said the little girl. 'At least, you could be.'

The ravens cawed and cawed and hopped about with laughter.

'We are your brothers? With our black feathers and long beaks. Haven't you heard that ravens bring bad luck? Brothers!'

'Caw, caw,' croaked the others, 'you are making fun of us.'

'Do you know where you were born?' the little girl asked them.

'Caw, caw, how should a raven know where it was born? Ask a better question.'

'My brothers were sent to fetch water for my christening from the well, and did not come back. My father wished them to be turned into ravens.'

'Caw, caw,' said the ravens, 'go on.'

'It is bedtime now,' said the little girl, 'Tomorrow morning I shall tell you the rest of the story.'

Before she went to her own bed, she helped the ravens into the splendid nightcaps the children from the end of the world had made them.

Even more difficult was to help the ravens on with their bed-socks, which looked like loose gloves tied on. It wasn't easy to fit them on over those strong horny claws.

The other children had already gone to their seven little beds—that is except for one who crept in beside her sister to leave a bed free for the little girl.

The little girl slept soundly and didn't hear a thing. But the next day the children told her that all night long they heard the ravens cawing and crowing on their perches on the backs of chairs.

The next morning, just as the sun was coming up over the edge of the world, the little girl was woken up by a raven standing by her bed.

'Caw, caw, little girl, come along. My brothers have sent me to get you out of bed. They want to hear the rest of your story, especially the parts about them. Caw, caw, do wake up. I mustn't come back without you.'

The little girl rubbed her eyes and stretched and tried hard to wake up.

Soon she was sitting on a bank outside the house. The ravens had hopped and jumped and flown about with high excitement from the moment she arrived.

Now she gathered them round her. She put her arms round them and caressed their shining black feathers, and their bony feathered heads.

The next morning the little girl was woken up by a raven standing by her bed.

*Tears poured down the
ravens' beaks . . .*

'Now go on with your story,' they said. 'We've been wanting to know more all night about you being our sister. How could that be?'

'You must tell me first all you can remember,' said the little girl. 'Do you remember my mother, who could be your mother too? A lady with a long gown and apron and a white headdress?'

The ravens seemed to be trying to remember but not quite succeeding.

'But what was that you said about your father turning us into ravens?' asked one of the birds.

'I was a weak newly born baby, and my brothers were sent to get water for my christening, because they thought I was going to die. And at the well . . .'

'I remember water,' said one, and the

others cawed in agreement.

'I have always, since I was told about it, felt very sad that it was because of me that my brothers had to go away from home, and perhaps be bewitched into ravens like you.'

'I know, unlucky birds.'

'Do you know this ring?' asked the little girl, pulling her mother's ring from her apron pocket. 'It belongs to my . . . our mother . . .'

'I'm sure I do.' The raven who took the ring in his beak passed it to the others. The diamond sparkled in the sun.

The ravens were beginning to understand and remember and tears poured down their beaks as she held them close.

But soon the ravens had their beaks mopped dry by the little girl and every one was smiling again.

One of them was still holding the diamond ring belonging to their mother in his beak.

'You know, we have a store of stones which flash and sparkle like this. If you come with us, we can show them to you.'

The little girl went with the ravens up a steep ladder into the attic. While she climbed the steps, the birds fluttered round her or hopped and flew from rafter to floor.

The raven pushed open the door with his beak and the little girl went inside into a room full of queer objects. The attic was dusty, and was the storeroom for trunks and boxes and other things put away in it and forgotten.

'We shall have to light a candle,' said the raven. 'There is a flint and tinder box over here, little girl, if you could use it for us. Ravens are not good at it.'

The little girl lit the candle and saw a raven open the door of an old grandfather clock. He pulled out a handkerchief and opened it. It was full of shining precious stones that seemed to be lit up from inside.

'Where did you get these?' she asked.

'Oh ravens collect sparkling stones,' he said. Among the stones was a ring.

'My mother's ring! A ring she said my brothers had with them for the baby when they disappeared. Now I know you must be my true brothers. You must come home with me and meet my father and mother and we shall tell them the story.'

The little girl helped them gather the precious stones into the handkerchief and knot them inside it tightly. Then she blew out the candle and went with the ravens back down the attic steps.

There were the children from the end

of the world who were only just waking up, yawning and stretching.

'Whatever are you all doing out of bed and off your perches so early?' they asked. 'Why, it's only just breakfast time.'

'I'm taking the ravens home with me,' the little girl told the children. 'I'm sure they are my brothers now.'

He pulled out a handkerchief and opened it. It was full of shining precious stones.

The ravens carried the little girl up to the sky on their wings.

The ravens carried the little girl on their wings. They flew with her right up into the sky and over the way across the world she had travelled to find them.

Soon they landed right outside the house with the apple tree.

Their mother embraced them tenderly. She was overjoyed to see them.

By chance a stone rolled out from the

handkerchief when the little girl was taking out the lost ring to show her mother.

One of the ravens took the stone in his his beak, and presto! there stood a boy. Soon all were restored. And so luck returned to their house.

Their mother was overjoyed to see them.

Aladdin and his Wonderful Lamp

In a big city in China there once lived a poor tailor whose name was Mustapha. Every day in his tailor's shop, Mustapha used to sit cross-legged on the floor, stitching and snipping fine suits for his customers. But he was never able to make much money no matter how hard he worked.

Mustapha and his wife had one son called Aladdin, who was quite different in his ways from his father. Aladdin was naughty and used to run out and play when he was supposed to be in school.

He would disobey his father often. If he said, 'Now, Aladdin, you must stay indoors and help us today,' when he and his wife came to look for him up and down the house and in the street, they would find he had gone out to play without telling them.

As sure as anything he had run away to games in the town square or in another part of the city with his friends. And these friends were as idle and bad as Aladdin.

It isn't surprising that Aladdin was a great worry to his parents. Nothing seemed to go right with him At school he did the worst work of anyone.

At last his father said to him, 'It is no good, Aladdin, you are wasting your time at lessons. Now you are older you can come and help me. I will teach you how to be a tailor, and that way we can earn more money, with two of us working, and have a better life.'

Aladdin, who was used to playing and getting up to mischief all day long, came reluctantly into the dingy little shop and sat cross-legged on the floor the way his father showed him.

His father tried to teach him how to push the needle in and out of the material and how to cut out the cloth, but Aladdin would not learn.

He spoilt precious cloth belonging to customers by cutting it out all wrong, and cost his father a lot of money. He fidgeted all the time he was supposed to be stitching. And if his father sent him out to take a suit to a customer when it had been finished, Aladdin nearly always took the chance to steal away and play.

Indeed he once went to play before he had delivered the suit and forgot the package. An old beggar found it and was delighted to find inside it a brand new suit of tunic and trousers which he sold for food.

You wouldn't think that a boy who gave so much trouble and looked like being even poorer than his parents, would end up the owner of a jewelled palace and married to a princess!

No matter how often the poor tailor

warned his son that one day he would be sure to be sorry for his lazy and selfish ways, Aladdin used to yawn in his face.

In the end, worn out and bent with worry, Mustapha became ill and died. Now there was no one to make Aladdin behave. His mother was much too soft-hearted to keep him in order.

Now he went out and played with his friends all day long. One day when he was in the street with some boys, a stranger passed by. He stopped and watched them for a long time, but they did not notice him. They nearly jumped three feet in the air when he spoke to them.

The stranger was a wicked wizard known as the African magician and he was looking for a boy to help him carry out a secret plan even the boy wouldn't know about.

He thought Aladdin looked like a

Aladdin's father tried to teach him how to become a tailor.

likely boy. The boys were rather afraid of the man with his cunning face and soft voice, but they let him send Aladdin to buy some cakes for them.

By the time Aladdin got back, like a

The boys were afraid of the man with his cunning face.

snake the magician had plied all the facts out of them that he wanted to know about Aladdin.

When the others left, munching the cakes, the African magician walked home with him.

'You aren't any relation of Mustapha the tailor, I suppose,' he asked him, putting an arm round his shoulder.

'Why, he was my father, but he's dead now,' said Aladdin.

'I knew it! You're so like him. He was my long-lost brother. So I am your uncle.'

A huge boulder with a ring in it rose from the earth.

The magician persuaded Aladdin's mother to believe in him so well, that before three days were out, she had allowed him to take Aladdin on a trip to the mountains.

He led the boy on a long journey being kind and loving to him all the way. Then when they came to the place he was secretly looking for, suddenly he stopped. He drew some signs in the dust and chanted strange words, a magic spell.

Instantly a huge boulder with a ring in it rose from the earth.

'Now,' said the magician, 'take hold of that ring and lift the rock up.'

'But uncle,' said Aladdin, 'I can't.'

'Only you can lift it,' said the magician, 'and if you do, you will find some steps under it which go down to a treasure house which will keep you and your mother in untold riches for ever.'

The magician's eyes glittered as he said this. The truth was he wasn't going to share any of it. Aladdin took hold of the ring and lifted the rock easily.

Aladdin took hold of the ring and lifted the rock easily.

There were the steps. The magician nudged Aladdin's arm eagerly.

'Go down my boy to the bottom of the steps, and you will come to three great caves one after another. In each cave are four brass urns filled with gold and silver. Do not touch them or anything else or let your clothes brush against them, or you will die.

'Go straight through the caves and through a door at the end. You will find a garden with fruit trees, but don't stop. Go straight across and take the lamp from the wall you'll see there, and bring it back to me.

'Wear this ring, it will protect you,' and he handed Aladdin his own ring.

Aladdin went down the rough-hewn steps.

Aladdin went down the rough-hewn steps. The boy's eyes opened wide when he entered the vast cave glittering with treasures, gold and jewels.

He passed through each cave in turn, carefully avoiding touching anything, or even letting his clothes brush against the wall.

He paused for a second at the fruit trees in the garden after the third cave. They were hung with huge jewels. His uncle hadn't mentioned these.

He crossed to the wall and felt some disappointment. The thing he was to bring back was only a battered oil lamp. He took it down, and put out the light.

Then he went back to the fruit trees and filled his tunic with jewels.

He went back to the trees and filled his tunic with jewels.

He picked as many as he could cram in his belt too, though the lamp tied to his belt was in the way.

Now Aladdin was afraid of his new uncle. There was something nasty about him, something dangerous.

'Come along, come along,' called the magician impatiently when at last Aladdin appeared on the steps again. Then, in case Aladdin began to suspect him, he said 'Your dear mother will be looking for us soon.'

Aladdin found it difficult to climb the stairs with both hands holding the jewels in his tunic and belt. He nearly toppled over several times.

'Give me the lamp,' said the African magician, stretching down his hand for it. 'Let me take the lamp.'

'Yes, uncle,' said Aladdin, 'I will give it to you, but first help me get out of this hole.'

The magician thought Aladdin was keeping the lamp purposely. He thought Aladdin had discovered somehow that it was a magic lamp. In the magic book where he had found out about the lamp, it said that the lamp would have to be given to him. He could not take it himself. He depended on Aladdin to hand it over.

So the wicked magician got angry with Aladdin and Aladdin couldn't make him understand that he needed help to climb out of the cave entrance.

'I'll give it to you,' said Aladdin, 'but first help me get out of this hole.'

Aladdin screamed and begged to be let out, but no one answered.

So the magician began to threaten Aladdin and scream with rage, and the boy began to cry.

'For the last time, will you give me the lamp?' shouted the magician.

'I can't uncle,' whimpered Aladdin.

'Then stay where you are for ever!' cried the magician, beside himself with fury. He pronounced a magic spell which made the entrance to the caves close over with Aladdin inside.

'Now keep the lamp and much good may it do you underground,' he hissed as he hurried away. 'I'll have to go back to Africa,' he muttered as he ran along, 'or else the silly people in that town will be wanting to know what I've done with Aladdin.'

Aladdin screamed and begged to be let out, but no one answered. After a time he calmed down and began to think what he ought to do. He obeyed the warning not to touch the walls of the cave or any of the gold, and sat down.

Aladdin sat at the foot of the steps, twisting the magician's ring on his finger anxiously.

Suddenly there was a huge puff of smoke and a gigantic genie rose out of it, and stood before Aladdin.

'I am the Slave of the Ring, O Master. What is your command?'

Aladdin couldn't speak for a minute, then he said, 'I want to get out of this place.' No sooner had he spoken than he found himself out on the mountain.

Suddenly there was a huge puff of smoke and a gigantic genie rose out of it.

172

'Where did you get this?' asked Aladdin's mother.

Aladdin had come out on a part of the mountain he did not know. There was no sign of the uncle that he now knew to be a magician.

The way back was wild and lonely, and Aladdin had a struggle to find food. He had to sleep beside rocks and in caves.

As he travelled this hard road, Aladdin began to feel ashamed of the selfish person he had been all his life. He resolved to be different when he got back to his own town.

After many days of travelling he at last opened the door of his mother's house. He found her very sad because she thought he must be dead, and poorer. She was spinning cotton to earn a living.

'No more of that now, mother,' he said, showing her one of the jewels. 'I shall

sell one or two of these and you shall live in luxury.'

'But where did you get this?' she asked.

Aladdin told her about the caves, the treasure—and the magician.

'Whatever this is worth,' said his mother replacing the jewel with the others, 'neither you or I, Aladdin, have a coin to buy supper with this night, and there isn't a crust in the house.'

She picked up the lamp.

'Now this is a battered old lamp, but it looks as if it is in working order. We could get some money for this is I polish it.'

So she fetched a duster and rubbed the lamp hard to make it shine.

She dropped the lamp with fright when from it curled up a column of smoke that grew larger and larger until it almost filled the little room. Out of the smoke appeared a mighty genie.

'I am the Slave of the Lamp,' he said, in echoing tones. 'What is your command, Oh Master?'

Aladdin had picked up the lamp. He held it to him and said:

'We are hungry. Bring us some food!'

The genie vanished and returned with a huge silver tray with twelve smaller dishes on it, all full of the most delicious food. Then he returned with bread and wine, enough for ten people for three days. All of this he did in a flash.

When the trays were empty, Aladdin sold them to a merchant. Soon he and his mother were wealthy. If ever they needed

'I am the Slave of the Lamp,' he said. 'What is your command, O Master?'

No one was allowed to look at the lovely Princess Buddir because she was the sultan's daughter.

anything, Aladdin had only to rub the lamp and the genie appeared. So time went by and Aladdin became a man.

One day the sultan's soldiers rode into town to order the people to stay indoors. The lovely Princess Buddir el Buddor was going to bathe, and no one was allowed to look on her because she was the sultan's daughter.

But Aladdin disobeyed so he could see her. She was even more beautiful than he had heard, and he instantly fell deeply in love with her and longed to marry her.

175

'The sultan would never allow his daughter to marry you,' said Aladdin's mother.

His mother asked him why he was so sad every day now.

'I have fallen in love with the sultan's daughter Princess Buddir el Buddor,' he sighed, 'and I wish—no I am determined to marry her.'

'But my son, even though you are now rich, you were born a tailor's son. The sultan would never allow his daughter to marry you,' said his mother.

'Perhaps with the help of the genie I may succeed,' said Aladdin. 'Mother, take these jewels to the sultan and tell him the rich and handsome young man who sent them wishes to marry his daughter.'

So Aladdin's mother waited every day at the palace, until the grand vizier said she could see the sultan.

'So you are the woman who has been waiting every day to see me,' said the sultan.

'My son has sent me with a gift of pearls for you, sire,' explained Aladdin's mother.

'So you are the woman who has been waiting every day to see me,' said the sultan. 'What is it you want of me?'

Aladdin's mother went down on her knees.

'O sire, I am here to speak for my son Aladdin who had the joy of seeing the face of your daughter, the Princess Buddir el Buddoor, and fell deeply in love with her.'

The sultan began to smile, but he did not interrupt.

'And he has sent me here with a gift of jewels for you, sire, and to tell you that he, Aladdin, a rich and handsome young man, would like to marry your daughter.'

The sultan was so surprised he broke into a wide grin, and then laughted, and so did the grand vizier and courtiers. But when Aladdin's mother uncovered the flashing jewels they gasped. These were

178

the jewels Aladdin had picked from the trees in the caves and they were as large as pigeons' and hens' eggs and seemed to radiate light from within.

The sultan took one of the jewels from the bowl and held it up to the light. Then he said, 'I am willing to consider the giver of the amazing jewels as a husband for my daughter when I have seen him.'

Aladdin was overjoyed at this news. 'Nothing shall prevent me marrying the beautiful princess,' he cried, and he took down the lamp and summoned up the genie.

'I am the Slave of the Lamp. What is your command, O Master?'

'I want to present myself to the sultan in such a way that he will let me marry his daughter.'

The genie vanished and returned with slaves, purses full of gold and jewels for the sultan, and a horse with gold trappings and silk clothes for Aladdin.

'Nothing shall prevent me marrying the beautiful princess,' cried Aladdin, taking down the lamp.

The princess fell as deeply in love with Aladdin as he had with her.

When Aladdin was shown into the room where the sultan was seated, he looked, with his gorgeous silk robes, as princely and handsome as any man.

Aladdin went forward, with a large number of his own servants following him, and knelt before the sultan. Then one after another his slaves went up to the throne and gave the sultan a purse of gold or a dish of jewels.

'This is an extraordinary and magnificent young man,' said the sultan in a whisper to the grand vizier. But the grand vizier began to hate Aladdin, because he hoped his own son was going to marry the princess.

But Princess Buddir el Buddor made her own choice. When she heard her servants talking about the wonderful suitor, so rich and graceful who had asked to marry her, she hid beside her window when he rode past on his horse with gold trappings.

As soon as she saw Aladdin she fell as deeply in love with him as he had with her. She went to her father and begged him to agree to the marriage. So the sultan gave his consent, and the wedding was quickly arranged.

But first Aladdin wished to prepare a palace in honour of his bride. He told the sultan what he wanted to do and the sultan gave him some land. Aladdin went back to his own house and took down the lamp and rubbed it.

At once the genie appeared.

'I am the Slave of the Lamp. What is your command, O Master?'

'Build me a palace for my bride,' said Aladdin, 'on the plot the sultan has given me. Have it ready in time for my wedding day tomorrow.'

By next morning the palace was ready. It was built of gold and silver and encrusted with jewels.

The wedding festivities lasted for a week and then Aladdin, who had been made a prince by the sultan, escorted his bride to the new palace.

She was carried on a litter surrounded by handmaidens and when she saw the glittering palace her hand went to her heart.

'Even the sultan my father's palace does not compare with this,' she gasped. And she and Prince Aladdin lived happily together and were loved by all the people for the many gifts they scattered among the poor.

But Aladdin had forgotten about the African magician, and one day that wicked sorcerer came back to China.

The magician knew at once that this Prince Aladdin must be the boy he had left shut in the treasure caves.

'He must have made the lamp serve him!' hissed the magician, when he saw the incredible palace in which Aladdin lived. He instantly formed a plot to obtain the magic lamp for himself.

He went to the market and bought a dozen new lamps, and then he waited about near the palace until he saw Aladdin go off hunting in the forest.

The magician walked under the window where he could see the princess

'New lamps for old. New lamps for old.'

The glittering palace vanished with all its inhabitants.

crying, 'New lamps for old. New lamps for old.' 'Why, we have an old lamp,' said the princess, to her maidservant, 'Prince Aladdin keeps it in his own rooms, I don't know why. I think I shall surprise him and put a new lamp in its place.'

The princess sent the maid down to bring up the man, little guessing that he was an evil magician. She went herself to bring the lamp from her husband's study.

When the African magician saw the lamp the princess was holding, he almost clapped his hands with delight. But he pretended to be indifferent as he gave her the new lamp in exchange.

As soon as he had possession of the lamp, he thrust it under his cloak and sped out of the palace so fast that the princess and her servants were startled.

He ran out of the town and into wild country, and did not take the lamp out until he was in a dark lonely wood. Then he rubbed it with his cloak.

Instantly the genie appeared.

'I am the Slave of the Lamp. What is your command. O Master?'

'Take up Prince Aladdin's palace, with the princess and all the servants and horses in it, and carry it to Africa.'

And in that instant the glittering palace and all in it vanished.

When the sultan next went over to admire the fantastic palace, as he often did, he rubbed his eyes. It had gone!

As Aladdin came back from hunting three days later, a troop of the sultan's soldiers rode out to arrest him.

'I give you forty days to bring back my daughter and her palace,' declared the angry sultan. 'I warn you Aladdin, return her or you will be beheaded.'

Aladdin wandered out of the city and sat by the river wondering what to do. While he was thinking he twisted the ring on his finger. Suddenly before him appeared the genie from the treasure cave.

'I am the Slave of the Ring, O Master. What is your command?'

'Bring me to my wife, wherever she is.'

And instantly Aladdin was transported to Africa under his wife's window.

When the princess told Aladdin about exchanging the lamps, he knew that she had been deceived by the magician.

He gave her some powerful poison and said, 'When he comes next, put this in the wine you offer him.'

She obeyed, and as soon as the magician tasted the drink he fell down dead.

Aladdin took back the lamp and called up the genie.

'Take this palace back to China as before.'

The sultan was overjoyed to see them, and with the magician dead, Aladdin and his wife lived happily ever after.

The next time the magician called on the princess she gave him poisoned wine.

The grasshopper laughed, 'Well, it is now. You won't catch me being such a fool. Let winter take care of itself.'

And the grasshopper went back to the other insects chuckling loudly, and started playing a jig on her violin, while the other creatures clapped their insect hands.

The summer passed slowly by and still the ant worked from morning till night. Her larder was filled to bursting, and she began to stop gathering and begin sorting her hoard into neat piles.

Now autumn came and the weather grew a little colder and the winds blew a little harder. But there were plenty of berries on the briars.

The grasshopper still found enough to eat, and although she was chilly now, she still sang and played the fiddle all day.

But the nights grew shorter. Soon the rain turned to snow and the berries were gone from the hedges. The squirrels had

taken all the acorns, and pigeons always reached any crumbs thrown out by humans first.

Soon the grasshopper began to feel so hungry it was quite unpleasant. Then she remembered the ant's larder.

'Isn't it lucky,' she said to herself, 'she'll be sure to have plenty of food to spare for me from that great store.'

And the grasshopper put on a warm scarf and hurried off through the snow to the ant's house, and knocked at the door.

'What can I do for you?' asked the ant.

'Ah, my dear mother ant,' said the grasshopper. 'Would you allow me to come in and warm myself and have something to eat? I have nothing at home and I know your larder is full.'

'Ah,' said the ant, 'I worked while you played, and you laughed at me then. Now let your violin find you food to eat. Sing and dance to keep yourself warm!'

The hungry grasshopper hurried off through the snow to the ant's house.

The Hare and the Tortoise

A hare one day sat boasting to the other animals in the wood.

'You know, I'm the fastest runner of all of you. In fact, I should think that I must be the fastest runner anywhere.'

And to show them what he meant he bounded round the field where they were talking.

The other animals nodded. There was no doubt about it. Not one of them could run anything like as fast as the hare.

'I'll tell you what,' said the hare, 'I challenge anyone to try and beat me in a race. I'd like to see if I really am the fastest.'

But none of the other animals spoke. They wouldn't have dared to challenge the hare. Only the tortoise sat thinking.

Like everything he did, the tortoise thought slowly. It wasn't until next day he said suddenly, when all the other animals had forgotten about the hare's challenge:

'I think I'll race against the hare!'

They were all so surprised that they burst out laughing.

'Race the hare? You? But Tortoise, running is not one of your strong points! If you race against the hare, who is fastest of us all, everyone will laugh!'

'I want to teach that boastful animal a lesson,' said the tortoise.

A procession of animals went to the hole where the hare lived. It was a slow journey because of the way the tortoise crawled.

'Mr Hare,' said the tortoise, 'I have come here to challenge you to a race.'

The hare looked at the tortoise and a grin spread over his face.

'You want to be a champion runner, eh, tortoise? If this isn't a joke, just tell me where the course is to be, and I'll be there.'

After his door closed the animals could hear him roaring with laughter. Now they went to find a judge. The tortoise said he would like the mole, who agreed to do it.

Everybody discussed where the race should be held. Then the mole announced:

'The race between the hare and the

The tortoise found the sun shining on his thick shell almost unbearably hot, but he never stopped once to rest or eat.

tortoise will be from the hollow oak, round the pond and back to the oak.'

The mole made the hare and the tortoise line up for the start.

'What's the prize?' asked the hare.

The mole thought and said, 'The loser gives the winner something nice to eat.'

'Now' he told the hare and tortoise, 'When I say, "*one, two, three, go!*" then you begin running. *One . . two . . three . . . go!*'

The hare began to run. In a few leaps he had reached the pond. All he had to do was race round it and back to the oak tree and he would be the winner.

The tortoise crawled out so slowly he hardly seemed to be moving at all. The hare felt a little hot and stopped to get his breath back. He looked behind him and saw that the tortoise had hardly gone a yard yet.

'Why should I wear myself out?' thought the hare, and as he was near his hole he went in to pick up a carrot.

He sat nibbling this and mocking the tortoise, when he began to feel sleepy. He lay back in the hedgerow, and dozed. The sun, high in the sky, warmed his fur and soon he was dreaming.

The tortoise found the sun shining on his thick shell almost unbearably hot. Drops of perspiration covered his forehead but he kept bravely on. He never stopped once to rest or eat.

The hare lay sleeping. The sun was setting when he woke up.

'I have something important to do. What is it?' and he jumped up. 'Why, it's to beat the tortoise in the race,' he cried and in a few bounds he ran round the pond and towards the oak tree.

But to his horror there was the tortoise just touching it with his nose.

Leap as fast as he could, the hare could not overtake him.

The tortoise was the winner. All the animals cheered and shouted at the crestfallen hare, who now had to give the tortoise the prize of a cabbage leaf. 'Slow and steady wins the race, hare.'

The hare had learnt his lesson. 'You must not only talk, but do.'

The Country Mouse and the Town Mouse

A fieldmouse met a town mouse out walking in the country, who stopped to ask the fieldmouse the way.

They stood chatting about the peace and beauty of the countryside, but all the time the fieldmouse could not take his eyes off the elegant red coat and yellow trousers the town mouse was wearing.

The town mouse noticed the way the fieldmouse's eyes kept glancing at his clothes and said, 'I see you admire the things I am wearing, my friend. They are the fashion in town just now. Maybe you would like to have some like them?'

'I certainly should like to!' said the fieldmouse enviously.

'Come with me to town then,' said the town mouse. 'I've got a fine waistcoat to spare hanging in my cupboard, and I think I could fit you out with some trousers too.'

The two mice walked along together talking in a friendly way until at last they came to the town.

The town mouse had told the fieldmouse that he lived in a splendid large house, and he had not exaggerated. It was furnished with luxury such as the fieldmouse had never set eyes on, with antique furniture and rugs.

On a side table stood dishes of sweets and an enormous chocolate cake.

'Have some,' said the town mouse. The fieldmouse by this time was very hungry because he had not eaten since breakfast.

While they were eating, between delicious nibbles, the town mouse told the fieldmouse about some of his adventures

'Come with me to town then,' said the elegant mouse.

'Quick, fly for
your life,' cried
the town mouse.

in town, escapes from cats, getting out of mousetraps and so on.

The fieldmouse had never eaten such lovely food or been in such a grand house, nor had he had any adventures to compare with the town mouse.

'What a marvellous life you have . . .' he began to say when suddenly his fur stood up on end. He heard a soft, 'Miaow . .' and saw a black shadow on the wall.

'Quick, fly for your life!' cried the town mouse, running down the table leg and into his hole. The fieldmouse raced after him and they both crouched in the hole together, trembling from head to toe.

When he had got enough breath to speak, the fieldmouse asked:

'Does the cat usually live round here?'

'Oh, yes,' said the town mouse, 'but I'm expert at escaping from his claws. You can see his eye there looking into the hole. We'll have to stay here till he goes away. Then there's some cheese on the kitchen dresser I'd like you to try, it's excellent quality.'

As the fieldmouse had been too polite to eat much of the chocolate cake while the town mouse was talking, he was still hungry and was glad when the town mouse said:

'The cat's gone. Now we can have that cheese.'

The fieldmouse had barely had time to get his teeth into the cheese when there was a sound of heavy footsteps. A woman had come into the room.

There was a piercing scream which froze the fieldmouse stiff with fright. 'Help! A mouse! No, two mice!' and the woman grabbed a broom and began whacking and thwacking at the mice as they ran for their lives.

'I bet you don't have adventures like this in the country,' said the town mouse,

'No, and I'm not sorry,' said the fieldmouse. 'I find this life too risky for me.'

So he set off home. The town mouse went part of the way. When they parted the fieldmouse said:

'If you want to dine in peace, come to me. It may be dull, but it's safe.'

'If you want to dine in peace, come to me,' said the fieldmouse. 'It may be dull, but it's safe.'

The Rabbit, the Weasel and the Cat

There was once a rabbit that every day at noon used to go for a long walk. When he was out one day he stumbled and sprained his ankle.

He found himself a stick and limped home feeling very sorry for himself. He had been gone for several hours, much longer than usual, and it was already getting dark when he arrived home.

To his surprise he saw that a light was burning in his living room.

'This is very odd,' said the rabbit.

He thought perhaps a friend had come to visit him, or perhaps a neighbour had called in to borrow some sugar.

He looked through the window and saw Mrs Weasel sitting in the most comfortable armchair close to the window.

Now Mrs Weasel was a very clever lady, and it was well known that she was fond of playing practical jokes on the other animals who lived in the wood.

The rabbit opened the door of his house and went inside.

'Good afternoon, Mr Rabbit,' said Mrs Weasel. 'I must say, I think it is rather impertinent of you to come into my house in this way. I can't remember having invited you.'

The rabbit thought at first that he had misunderstood her. Her house? Dumbfounded he looked about him. All his furniture had gone and Mrs Weasel's was in its place.

'Y-y-your house?' he managed to say at last. 'My house, you mean. I inherited this house from my parents! Your house? I like a joke as well as anybody, but this is going too far. I must ask you to leave immediately. I should not like to forget you are an old lady and throw you out.'

Mrs Weasel did not shrink under this threat. Indeed, she laughed very loudly.

'Why should I want to go away? I'm sitting here very comfortably, and there is plenty of food in the larder.'

'But I saved that food for myself,' stammered Mr Rabbit. He was be-

'Do come in, my
dear friends,'
said Mr Cat.

wildered by her cool impudence. 'You can't just walk into another animal's house like this, madam.'

'My dear Mr Rabbit,' said Mrs Weasel, 'that I can. I can prove it to you,' and she picked up a book from the table and waved it at him.

'This is the Animal Housing Manual,' she said. 'In here it states that if any animal enters a house without a master in it, he may live there.

'I find it very inconvenient that this house is so small. If it was larger I might have been able to ask another woman to share it with me and she would have paid me a reasonable rent. But if you don't want to pay me yourself you must go.'

And she pushed the rabbit out of the house and slammed the door after him.

The rabbit was shocked and furious and battered at the door.

'Come out, weasel! You thief! Others shall hear about this.'

Then Mrs Weasel opened the window and said pleasantly with a smile:

'Mr Rabbit, don't let us quarrel like this. Let us go and take the problem to Mr Cat who lives at the Cat's House.'

The rabbit agreed. He was certain that the cat would take his side. But Mrs Weasel was sure he would take her side.

A quarter of an hour later they stood outside the cat's house. Mrs Weasel banged on the door. Before she had finished knocking the door opened and the cat looked out.

'What a pleasure!' he said. 'The fair Mrs Weasel and delightful Mr Rabbit. How charming of you to visit me. Do come in, my dear friends.'

'No, Mr Cat, thank you,' said Mrs Weasel. 'We want you to judge a problem.'

'It's about my house,' they both said, and then they each began to tell their own story at once and stood arguing.

'I'm afraid I can't hear what you're saying out here,' said the cat, and led them into his house still arguing.

And with a spring he ate them up; and solved their problem once and for all.

The cat solved their problem once and for all!

The Snow Queen

There was once a wicked troll, the devil in fact, who made a looking glass. Anyone who looked in this glass saw not a reflection of himself, but his eyes twisted and much enlarged.

If he was kind, it made him look ugly, and if he had a freckle it seemed to cover half his face. The finest scenery looked like spinach in this devil's mirror.

The devil and his troll friends had fun holding their looking glass up in front of human beings. Then one day they decided to fly up to heaven and to amuse themselves by holding the mirror up to the angels.

But as they flew close to heaven the mirror began to quiver and shake, and in sight of the angels it broke into hundreds of millions of pieces which fell to earth.

Some of these pieces of glass got into people's eyes, so that they saw everything crooked and bad. Worse still, some of them got into people's hearts and stuck there, and made their hearts turn into lumps of ice and lose their feelings.

And when this happened, the friends of the person whose eyes saw everything distorted thought he'd just become sharper tempered. And sometimes if the glass was in his heart friends knew that something was wrong, but they couldn't say what.

This happened to somebody in this story and there was a world of trouble and tears before it was put right.

In a large town where the houses and people were crowded so close together that hardly anybody could have a garden, lived a poor little boy and girl whose garden was no bigger than a flower-pot.

The boy's name was Kay and the girl's was Gerda, and although they were not brother and sister they loved each other as dearly as if they were.

Gerda lived with her mother and father at the top of a tall old house, and Kay lived with his grandmother in the attic opposite.

The gables of the two houses were so close together they almost touched. Outside the windows were wooden boxes where the families grew herbs. In each box was a rose tree. Then the two families had an idea.

'Why don't we put those boxes across the space between the houses like a little bridge of flowers!' In summer the plants trailed across from one house to the other.

The two children were not allowed to climb across by these boxes, but they were allowed to sit out in the sunshine on their little stools and talk.

In summer Kay and Gerda were only a couple of yards apart. But in winter, when the windows were shut and covered with ice, they had to run all the way downstairs and into the street, then up the stairs of the other house so they could be together.

Sometimes they used to heat a copper

coin on the stove and then press it against the glass. The ice used to melt and then there was a peephole to look out at the world outside.

Kay and Gerda could see just one eye of each other at this tiny round window. Outside the snow was piled up on the flower-boxes and the gutters and snow-flakes fell down thick and large.

'They look like white bees swarming,' said Kay to his old grandmother, 'do they have a queen like the bees?'

'Oh yes,' said his grandmother, 'the Snow Queen flies in the middle of the snowflakes and breathes ice flowers on the windowpane. But when the wind comes she goes back into the black clouds.'

'Yes, we've often seen that,' said Kay and Gerda (who was visiting him).

That night Kay climbed up to the window and looked out to see if he could see the Snow Queen. While he was watching some of the snowflakes seemed to collect together and change into a woman.

Her long gown made of powdered snow was like white gauze glittering with snowflakes, and her eyes were ice-cold. Then a shadow passed like a bird.

The next day there was a frost but by midday the weather had changed and spring came back. The swallows returned to nest in the eaves, and Gerda and Kay sat talking together, and playing by the flowers outside their window boxes.

One afternoon, the two children were sitting looking at a picture book, when suddenly Kay said 'Ow!' and then, 'Ouch!' Just at that moment the clock on

Her long gown was made of powdered snow glittering with snowflakes, and her eyes were ice-cold.

the church tower struck five.

'What's the matter, Kay darling?' asked Gerda, putting her arms round him.

'Oh nothing,' he replied, 'I just had a sharp pain in my eyes and then another pain in my chest.'

But it was not 'nothing'. You remember the devil's looking glass? That mirror that was broken when the devil held it up to the angels. Some splinters from it had hit Kay.

Two small specks had gone into his eyes and a large silver had pierced his heart and changed it to a lump of ice. Now instead of seeing everything as it really was, Kay could only see ugliness.

He reached out and pulled two roses

The winter returned—and with it the snowflakes.

off the tree in the window box.

'Worm-eaten crooked old things!' he cried.

'Why Kay, what's the matter? What has happened to you?' asked Gerda anxiously.

'And this picture book is only for a baby like you to read!' said Kay.

After this he began to tease Gerda though she had always been his best friend, but she still loved Kay.

The winter returned and with it the snowflakes. Kay studied them through a magnifying glass and showed Gerda the wonderful shapes they formed. Each snowflake was like a flower or a ten-pointed star.

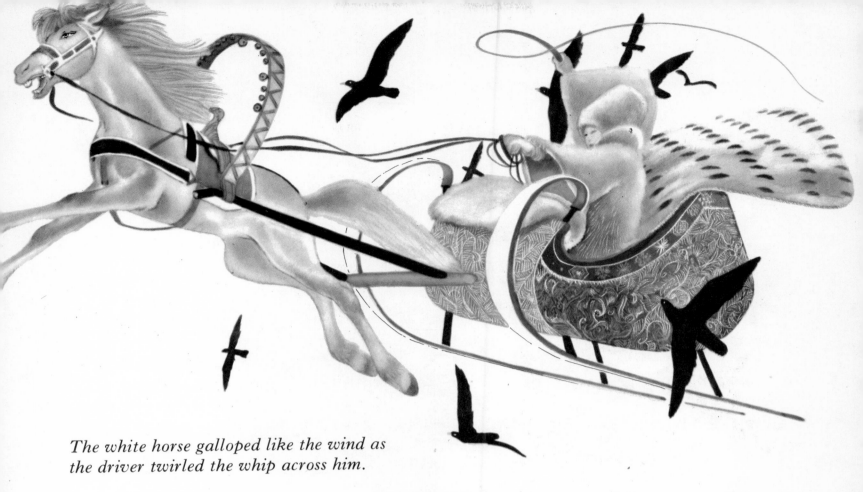

The white horse galloped like the wind as the driver twirled the whip across him.

'Aren't they lovely?' Kay said. 'More perfect than flowers except that they melt.'

Soon he came to Gerda all dressed up in his clothes for tobogganing. He was wearing a warm knitted hat and woollen mittens and a thick quilted jacket, and was carrying his little sledge.

'I'm old enough to go sledging with the big boys now, in the square,' he said. 'So I'm going to be off with them. Good-bye Gerda.'

The greatest fun was when the boys tied their sledges behind the farm carts so they could be pulled along for miles, with luck.

Kay was standing watching when a large white sleigh passed, driven by a woman in white furs who cracked her whip and drove twice round the square.

Kay managed to fasten his little sledge to the back of the sleigh and sped away through the streets of the town and out into the country.

The white horse galloped like the wind as the driver twirled the whip across him again and again. Kay felt frightened as his sledge flew up and bounced across ditches faster and faster.

Then the sleigh stopped.

'Come in beside me, Kay,' said the woman who had been driving the sleigh.

She helped him up and gave him two ice-cold kisses. With her kisses he completely forgot Gerda and his old grandmother, and his life so far.

'I shan't kiss you again,' she said. 'My kisses could freeze you to death. And she turned the sleigh north.

She was the Snow Queen. Kay realized her white furs were all made of snow.

When Kay did not come back everybody searched for him anxiously. The other boys could only say that they had

The flowers in the old woman's garden always puzzled Gerda.

seen him tie his sledge to a white sleigh and drive away after it. In the end everyone thought he must be dead.

But Gerda could not forget Kay. One day in spring she decided to go in search of him. As most people had thought Kay had probably been drowned, the first place she went to was the river.

She stood on the bank and took off her new red shoes. She threw them into the water and called out, 'If you took Kay away, bring him back and you can keep these red shoes.'

But the shoes were washed back to the bank. The river did not want them. Gerda picked them up and climbed into a boat that was tied up among the reeds. She undid the mooring and was floated along moving faster and faster on the current in the wild waters.

'Please river, take me to Kay,' she said, but it let her drift along.

An old woman on the bank saw the boat floating along the river with a little girl alone in it.

'Here,' she called out, 'I'll help you, little one.'

She stretched out the handle of her walking stick and hooked it over the prow of the boat. Then she pulled it into the side and helped Gerda out.

'Now who are you, little girl?' she asked. 'And tell me how you got into this trouble.'

Gerda explained that she was looking for her friend Kay, and told her about the window boxes and the rose trees.

The old woman listened kindly, but when Gerda was sitting on the fur rug eating some cherries she had given her, the old woman crept into the garden and pointed her walking stick at the roses to make them disappear.

She was not so much a witch as a woman who could do magic, and she longed to keep Gerda for her own little girl.

She thought that if Gerda saw roses they would remind her of Kay and leave her. That was why she made them vanish.

'I've always wanted a little girl like you,' she said while she combed Gerda's hair. As she combed Gerda forgot why she had come and about all the people she used to know.

The flowers in the old woman's garden always puzzled her. There was every kind but one. What was it? Then Gerda saw the roses painted on the old woman's hat and she remembered Kay.

'I must go to Kay,' she cried, and ran out of the garden and on her way. She went as far as she could, then had to rest.

A big crow flew down beside her.

'I'm looking for a handsome boy with long hair,' she said. 'He is called Kay.'

'Kay?' The crow put its head on one side. 'Yes, I've seen someone like that. He's going to marry the princess.'

Gerda followed as the crow flew before her to the castle, where the princess was going to wed, but when the bridegroom turned round, though he was handsome and had long hair, he was not Kay.

When the princess and her prince heard her story, they gave her a carriage to ride in, drawn by two jingling horses.

Gerda was grateful and drove the horses clip-clopping along the road, searching for Kay. But alas, soon she came to a forest where robbers lived. They jumped out from the trees with long knives and took Gerda back to their robber lair. If it had not been for a little robber girl Gerda would never have escaped.

The woman let them share some fish she was cooking.

'Listen,' she whispered to Gerda, when the robbers were asleep, 'My pet wood pigeon told me that Kay has been taken by the Snow Queen beyond the Northern Lights. I'll lend you my reindeer to carry you there. He'll lead you to a Lapp woman I know in Lapland, and she'll tell you where to go next.'

The little robber girl helped Gerda on to the back of the reindeer.

'Keep your arms round his neck,' she said, 'or you'll fall off.'

Gerda waved and the reindeer bounded away. They travelled always towards the north over plains and through forests. In the sky they could see flashes of light and the sky was bright.

'Those are the Northern Lights,' the reindeer called back over his shoulder. 'They say they are the Snow Queen's fireworks.'

They arrived at the house of the Lapp woman. It was a poor little hut, but the woman was kind and let them share some fish she was cooking. She told them:

'A Finnish woman I know can help you more than I can. She lives only two miles away from the Snow Queen's palace. Just give her this message I've written on a piece of dried codfish and she'll help you.'

'Thank you . . . thank you . . .' floated back on the Arctic wind as Gerda and the reindeer rode on to Finland.

'Kay is in the Snow Queen's power,' said the Finnish woman, 'I do know that. Two miles further on the wall round the Snow Queen's palace begins. Put the girl down by the red berry bush, reindeer, and wait for her.'

With the help of the angels Gerda got passed the Snow Queen's bristling snowflake sentries. The Snow Queen was away.

Kay lay frozen when Gerda found him, and he did not know her. She pressed her face on his chest and began to weep hot tears. They melted the ice in his

Gerda and the reindeer rode on to Finland.

heart and washed out the sliver of glass.

He began to revive. He opened his eyes.

'Gerda, it's you!' and he began to cry.

The tears washed the specks of glass out of his eyes. Now he could see. 'Where were you for so long, Gerda?' he asked. 'Let's go home now.'

'Yes,' said Gerda. 'Let's go home.'

Nawarana and the Giant

In cold Greenland there once lived an Eskimo woman called Nawarana, in a little village where most of the people were her friends and relations.

Everyone thought that Nawarana had a most difficult husband. He had a quick temper and was often angry with her.

Quite a lot of the time he was a pleasant and amusing man. But O woe, if anything upset him! Then he would shake his fist and bellow, and before you knew it had flown into a terrible fury.

Usually Nawarana was understanding, and managed not to set off her husband's temper. And if she spoke calmly back, he soon became nice again.

But if he really got into a rage, he would roar at her, and grip the handle of his huge knobbly club and chase her out of the house.

Luckily Nawarana could run much faster than her husband, and she always outstripped him. By the time he had caught up with her he was so out of breath his anger had gone.

'Next time,' said Nawarana, 'I shall do something about his ill treatment of me.'

She didn't have long to wait. On the following evening all the people saw Nawarana flying through the village with her husband on her heels.

But this time Nawarana did not return.

She headed out across the tundra, a bare and frozen land without any hills, where the wind blew howling and sighing and snow often fell in blizzards.

For two days and nights Nawarana trudged on. She became so hungry that at one time she stopped and crammed a

handful of snow into her mouth.

'If I don't find a shelter soon,' said Nawarana, 'I shall freeze to death. And I must find some food, or I shall die of starvation.'

The mountains ahead of her looked like the outstretched fingers of an enormous hand. Nawarana began to climb up the lower slopes and found a hollow sheltered from the wind. In here she curled up and fell deeply asleep.

The next day she climbed up a steep slope and on to a smooth flat plateau. She walked for the whole day, still with no food and weak from hunger.

She stumbled forward. Then she saw that ahead was a thick black wood.

Suddenly Nawarana stood stiff with fright as a deep voice like thunder boomed:

'Who are you and what are you doing in this place where no man ever comes?'

At first Nawarana could not speak and at last she said trembling, looking round everywhere:

'I am Nawarana. And who are you? Are you a mountain ghost?'

'No. I am a giant,' said the voice, and my name is Kinak. I live here on this vast plain so that I can stretch out when I sleep without crushing whole villages.'

'But where are you?' asked Nawarana. 'You are on me,' answered the giant. 'You climbed over my head, then up my arm and along my shoulder. You have been climbing over me for two days.'

'Oh!' cried Nawarana. 'I hope I haven't hurt you!'

There was a sound like a gale and a rumbling under her feet. Nawarana almost blew away. Then she realized the giant was laughing.

'I caught sight of you yesterday running across my wrist,' said Kinak, 'or I shouldn't have known you were there. If I had turned over you would certainly have been crushed. But what are you doing here, wandering alone?'

'I live in a comfortable house in a friendly village,' said Nawarana, 'but my husband used to chase me with a stick. Otherwise I should never have left home.'
'And what are you going to do now?'
'Perhaps I could stay with you, Kinak?'

'Very well,' said the giant, 'climb by my beard and look for a place on my face

Nawarana headed out across the tundra, a bare and frozen land.

to camp. Somewhere above my mouth so I won't swallow you by mistake.'

Nawarana began to climb, holding on to the hairs in his skin for support.

'Now I must get you something to eat.'

The sky darkened and there was a huge shadow across it. Nawarana screamed, then realized it was Kinak. He gave her some steak and reindeer hides for a tent.

Nawarana lived on Kinak's face for a few weeks. She made a tent from the hides he gave her, and a jacket and new boots, and lived on reindeer steak. One day Nawarana sighed deeply and Kinak heard her.

'Are you homesick?' he asked.

'Yes, Kinak, it's silly but I'd like to show my reindeer boots to my husband, and my new jacket to all my neighbours.'

'You've a lot to pack, but I'll help you, and carry you home.'

'Why, do you want me to go?' asked she. 'The truth is I'm getting stiff because I dare not turn over with you on my face,' said the giant, and Nawarana laughed.

Soon the hides were tied in a roll on her back. The giant told Nawarana to climb on his underlip.

Then he blew hard. It was like a hurricane! Nawarana flew through the air and landed at her own front door.

'Where have you been?' roared her husband reaching for his club at once.

'Kinak! Kinak!' she cried, 'Help me!'

At that instant there was a gust of wind that blew her husband upside down.

'I think you are friends with a ghost,' he said, scrambling up. But Nawarana smiled and said nothing. Since then the club has not come out.

At that instant there was a gust of wind that blew her husband upside down.